NO LAUGHING MATTER

Kurt M. Criscione

About the O. C. L. T. Series

There are incidents and emergencies in the world that defy logical explanation, events that could be defined as supernatural, extra-terrestrial, or simply otherworldly. Standard laws do not allow for such instances, nor are most officials or authorities trained to handle them. In recognition of these facts, one organization has been created that can. Assembled by a loose international coalition, their mission is to deal with these situations using diplomacy, guile, force, and strategy as necessary. They shield the rest of the world from their own actions, and clean up the messes left in their wake. They are our protection, our guide, our sword, and our voice, all rolled into one.

They are O.C.L.T.

TALES OF THE O. C. L. T.

AVAILABLE NOW:

Brought to Light: An O.C.L.T. Novella by Aaron Rosenberg
The Temple of Camazotz: An O.C.L.T. Novella by David Niall Wilson
The Parting: An O.C.L.T. Novel by David Niall Wilson
Lost Things by Melissa Scott & Jo Graham

UPCOMING:

The Highjump: An O.C.L.T. Novel by David McIntee
Schrodinger's Tomb: An O.C.L.T. Novel by David Niall Wilson
Digging Deep: An O.C.L.T. Novel by Aaron Rosenberg

I started sifting through the coal and ash at the bottom of the fire pit, pushing aside lengths of charcoal and less identifiable lumps. One looked like it might have been a waxed paper cup, another looked like an empty condom foil, and still another might have been a melted spork.

I didn't know what I expected to find. I seriously doubted I would dig down and uncover a leering skull, and yet every time I pushed the ashes aside, that was exactly what I expected.

I reached the stone-lined bottom and sighed. It was more of nothing. I widened the hole in the ash and found two lumps of metal. I threw the stake aside and reached into the pit. There was still some residual warmth in the stones and I picked up the black lumps. I rubbed them in my palm and a bright sheen was revealed. Silver?

I dove into the ashes with my gloved hands, scooping away ashes and shoving them hurriedly to the edge of the pit. My jacket was soon covered in pale ash and a cloud above me clearly marked that I was trespassing on private property. I didn't care.

I found a skull. Thankfully not the one I feared to find, but it was just as damning. It was a silver skull and crossbones, the edges of the bones having melted from the heat, along with the other two lumps I'd already found. I was certain that these three pieces were what remained of the piercings that had adorned Jacob Carpenter's face.

Acknowledgments

First I want to thank David Niall Wilson and not just for giving me a chance with this book, but for being my friend. He was the first author to ever talk with me as a peer and not just as a fan. Even going so far as to give me his email address and phone number and always have time for me. He is just good people.

Second, I want to thank Jon Sales; friend, pre-reader, and the basis for Jon Shaw… sorta mostly kinda… ha. Thanks for always being excited by my stories and always asking for more.

Brian Keene for giving me a forum that allowed me to come out of my shell and meet a ton of great people, and for inspiring me to pull out the keyboard and start writing again.

James Moore for the great bear hugs, the NECON memories, and for the threats that keep me writing.

Rick Hautala for being a great guy and for always having extra rum.

Also all the new friends I've made over the last three years be they writers, readers, horror fans, some of which are impatiently asking when this book will be available: TTZuma, David Dodd, Paulo, Chris J, Susan S, Matt B, Mike A, Nanci K, Thad, Craig, Xavier M, Tom E, Skip, Paula and Mark B, and so many others.

And all my family, blood and extended and adopted, especially the people who just leave me alone at my computer and sometimes bring me dinner, because they know I just want to get a 10K day. Thanks everyone.

Cover by Dave Dodd
Design by Aaron Rosenberg
ISBN 978-1-948929-34-9

 For information address Crossroad Press at 141 Brayden Dr., Hertford, NC 27944
www.crossroadpress.com

First edition

This book is dedicated to David Paul Miron. He was a second father to me and he took me into his home when times were tough. He never stopped believing in me or my dreams, even when I had stopped believing. The way he would always ask when he would have a book on his shelf with my name on the spine. I wish he was still here to see this now, but I know he's watching over me.

Author's Note

I used a bunch of real places throughout this book and a bunch of made up places as well. First and foremost, I just want to say that I do NOT know any of the Litchfield Police and they are in NO way as pictured in this book. I've taken liberties with a bunch of places and if you happen to live in any of them, please just let it go. Some of the places are only named because friends and family are there and I wanted them to get a chuckle.

Thank you for reading.

1

Third time's the charm. Whoever had made that adage up didn't have trips to the hospital in mind. This is my third in less than a year and while I can admit to a certain amount of clumsiness, they were not all my fault.

My father has just left the room and given me a lot to think about. Despite that I'm nearing thirty, I still love, respect, and fear my father. The worry and disappointment in his eyes hurts more than broken ribs or the stab wounds. The words he left me with ring in my skull. *Boy you trying to kill yourself? You have some kind of death wish? What the hell is so important you keep ending up in this place? Talk to me.* His slight Kansas boy accent making his voice softer as he got madder. With my father it was the quiet you had to be afraid of; he was not a shouting man.

I didn't know what to say. I could tell he didn't believe me when I told him I wasn't suicidal. A nurse interrupted our stare down; the tension in the room, filling it like a balloon full of super-heated air, deflated as she entered and told my father that visiting hours were over.

I really did want to tell him the truth but I also didn't want to be committed to the psych ward. The last year has been a nightmare, figuratively and literally. My beliefs have been turned upside down and left for dead. These are all I could think of, these… stories, case files? Yeah case files. These files will only contain the truth. As close as I can tell what the *truth* is, it will be written here. They are meant for the eyes of First Sergeant Charles Shaw, my father, so that in the case of my death, he might be apprised of what was so important.

I guess that was a long winded… preamble. But it helps me to put my thoughts in order. Where does one begin? They always say start at the beginning but actually I should probably introduce myself. Just in case a cop finds these files or perhaps some stranger cleaning out my house.

My name is Jonathan Charles Shaw and I'm a private investigator… and a gunsmith… and sometimes bodyguard. To be honest, I'm somewhat "attention challenged". I've been a lot of things much to the chagrin of my father. I will readily admit that sometimes I allow my dreams to steer me instead of reality. In high school I wanted to be a chef and while I took culinary classes and worked in kitchens, I won't be appearing on any shows on Food TV. I worked as a mechanic, a shipper, and I stayed in college part time throughout. Heck, I earned a bachelor's in business management and certificates in tons of things ranging from accounting to computer networking to Criminology.

Like I said I tended to flit from subject to subject as the whim took me. I took nothing seriously and had to tolerate being called "Kid" by all my friends, and most of my family. There was one thing I did take seriously and that was the martial arts. I've practiced Aikido for over fifteen years and Kenjutsu for the last seven.

Warrior tradition. My father is a career Marine. As a boy I wanted to follow his footsteps, but he was pretty adamant that he didn't want his son in the military. Especially not with the current state of affairs in the Middle East. He'd been deployed four times over the last nine years and every time he returned he told me he was glad he hadn't allowed me to enlist at eighteen.

If he only knew the war I was in now.

But that's getting ahead of myself. After eight years of college I had earned my degree and decided to go into business for myself. My first idea was a computer repair shop and that was ok, but then this bodyguard job fell into my lap. I live in rural Connecticut and believe it or not, there are a lot of stars hiding around the area. You know the saying, "look before you leap"? Well, apparently I don't. I took the job and ended up running around Boston and New York as a bodyguard for a celebrity who will remain nameless. I got into some fancy parties and I got to dress up like a Secret Service man, wearing a suit with my pistol in a shoulder holster; it was exciting.

I closed down my computer repair business and ran around for a month having a great time. I then envisioned my new bodyguard/ personal security company as my ticket to success. That was a bust, so I'll just skip to the punch line. Having a friend hook you up with a one-time great job is no basis for a company of your own. By the time I tried to backpedal and restart my computer business, I'd been snookered. Another shop had opened a few miles down the road, all my customers had gone.

This is depressing. But it's the beginning of the story. The story of my first time in the hospital, last fall. We'll just rush through the next little bit.

I decided to fold the bodyguard business into a new venture. Gunsmithing. Shooting and hunting has been a part of my life since I was child and not to stroke my own ego, but I'm a damn good shot. I took some lessons, apprenticed to a gunsmith and got my licenses. From there I expanded my business. The house I owned was zoned both commercial and residential so I converted the basement to a work shop, half the ground floor to a gun store, the other half to my offices, and the upstairs into my home.

Business was good again. With the war and the economy sinking into the proverbial pit, guns were selling, and if not new guns, then the folks wanted their old ones looked at and fixed.

As stated earlier I'm attention challenged so of course I had to *spice up* the business. My last failed venture was Big Game Hunting. I was going to organize trips and lead them into the wilderness. I was thinking Moose and Bear in Alaska and Canada. Some of my first clients were thinking more like lions in Africa, so that never worked out. Luckily I had just gotten my certificate in Criminology, and since I was filing paperwork for my explosive licensing anyway, it turned out to be just a form and a fee to get my PI license.

Which I guess, in a long winded way, brings us to last summer and my first job as a PI. It also brings us to my first visit to the hospital.

2

Erin Carpenter was my first client and while I know it's prob-ably a cliché to have a hot woman walk in and set the *gumshoe* on a case, one, this is exactly how it happened and, two, this isn't a 1940s noir movie.

I can only imagine what was going through Erin's mind as she stepped onto my porch. I have a long porch that runs across the entire front of the house, the kind of place you'd sit with a pitcher of lemonade or sweet tea and smile to the neighbors. It's a big house that would probably be more at home in the south. The front windows are covered with posters, similar to the Movie Theater Lobby posters in size and style. The one just to the left of the front door is a bit of a joke, an advertisement from my failed hunting company. It's dominated by a stylized picture of myself with an old English pith helmet, khakis, and a huge rifle on my shoulder. I have my foot up on the carcass of a huge bear, Captain Morgan Style. Across the top of the poster it says: JON SHAW and along the bottom: MONSTER HUNTER.

I have to admit I loved the cheesiness of it. At the time, it was just a joke; I'd used the word "monster" to replace extreme, or large. I liked the play on words, and now—in hindsight—I wish I had never had it commissioned. Who knew how true the *joke* would be.

The fact that, after seeing it, Erin still decided to enter the building was a tribute to how desperate she was. Or maybe she just had blinders on. The front door was a huge ancient oak affair that I tried to make welcoming with mats and signs saying to please enter.

The foyer was a small room, six by eight, with doors on the left and right walls. Straight ahead I had coat racks, an antique bench, a mat for muddy boots, and a couple of stands with umbrellas in them.

The door on the right said SHAW FIREARMS while the one on the left said SHAW INVESTIGATES. Both of these doors appeared to be more oak, but were in fact solid steel with an oak veneer. The entire foyer was actually a steel box. Some say paranoid, others say prudent.

I saw her on the monitor on my desk and triggered the left hand door before she could reach for it. The door buzzed and opened into the room a handbreadth. Erin paused, sighed deeply, then opened the door and stepped into my office.

Again imagining what she thought as she entered. She saw a large open room with a massive fireplace on the north wall. The south wall was dominated by a lacquered display case, twelve feet wide, bookended by a suit of recreated samurai armor and a suit of heavily padded Kendo armor. The display case held drawers and a shelf displaying the *Diasho*, in the Miyamoto tradition two katana instead of the normal katana and wakazashi.

It was a beautiful and impressive set-up, more so if you knew the money involved in creating it, but I had little faith that she even knew what it was. Her eyes traveled the room, not really noticing anything beyond the large desk, centered between the north and south walls and closer to the foyer door, and me. I didn't like making people cross the entire width of the room, so my back was to mostly empty space. A small couch and a practice mat, more a decorative rug than a practical piece of equipment, were all that filled the area behind my desk.

She sort of stutter-stepped as she neared the chair across from me. I knew it was my appearance. I'm tall and lean, my face baby smooth, and I'm sure she was thinking I was fresh out of high school, instead of a decade removed. I wore a suit, but casually, the jacket draped over a chair, no tie, the top two buttons open on my shirt, and an empty shoulder holster in plain sight. I held out my hand and Erin had the good grace to take it, I clasped her hand in both of mine. I was hoping that the firmness of my grip and the calluses on my palms would convey my age and experience better than my looks.

She let out a shaky breath and I let her go, gesturing toward the chair as I took my own seat. I took that moment to size her up. Erin was small, barely over five feet, brunette, blue-eyed—always a stunning combo—and thin, in an athletic, not skinny, way. I pegged her as younger than me by a handful of years, until I looked at her eyes up close. They were bloodshot and red rimmed. She'd been doing a lot of crying and I could just make out a touch of makeup covering incipient crow's feet.

Her hair was styled, her jeans were designer, her hands manicured, and her blouse nice. She wore comfortable shoes, well worn, most likely a runner which explained her build and light step. She sank into the chair and rubbed her hands together. I couldn't help but notice the mark where a wedding ring had been.

"Mrs. Carpenter," I began.

"Miss. But just call me Erin," her voice was tired, just above a whisper, but loud enough so I didn't need to lean across the desk to hear her.

"Erin, then. First off, let's just dismiss the appearance of my age. I know how I look and I assure you that it's just a look I cultivate. It's helpful to be underestimated in my line of work."

"You need a young face to sell guns and make posters?"

I grinned at her and was pleased to see a flash of a smile in return.

"I also bodyguard and make a killer burger," I got another smile out of her. "But you're not here to help me launch a failed career as a comedian. You're here because you either need protection, or you need me to find something."

She looked puzzled for a second and I flipped a thumb over my shoulder toward a picture of me in Secret Service get up and my one and only A-list celeb client. Her eyes widened.

"Is that…?"

"Yes it is, but something tells me you're not here looking for a bodyguard. Why don't you tell me what I can do for you?"

Erin took a deep breath and then reached into a small purse I had failed to notice. I would berate myself later for noticing the shoes and manicure but not the purse. She pulled out a picture and stared at it.

"My son has gone missing. The police are calling it a runaway and telling me I need to wait a few more days. They aren't doing anything." She threw the picture on the desk and pulled a napkin out of her purse.

I looked the picture over as she wept. Crying women always upset me and I felt myself getting angry. I had no target for the emotion and it frustrated me. I looked at the picture. The kid appeared to be in his late teens. I had to reassess Erin's age by about a decade, unless she had the boy when she was twelve.

I'd expected some skinny emo kid, the breed currently running around the middle and high schools, but this kid was a throwback to a different era. He looked like late seventies punk crossed with biker and leather-clad head-banger. He wore a leather jacket with a jean vest covered in band patches from the 80s. His hair was shaved on the sides and spiked on top, he had a high school goatee, and he was pierced. A giant skull and crossbones hung from his ear, pulling the lobe down, and two silver rings pierced his right nostril. He was sneering at the camera, a lot of anger in his eyes, the same blue as his mother's.

Erin recovered, "Not the best picture but the most current. His father died a few years back and he's been a handful ever since. I told him he could get his ear pierced and he came back with a face full of metal. I really don't know what went wrong. I won't blame the music or his friends or any of that. I know it's the loss of his father and teenage hormones. I know that my son was mad and I know he likes to run out, but I also know he loves me and he wouldn't just leave. He's been gone for the entire weekend, three days, and still the cops are saying he'll come back."

I flipped the photo over, unable to meet her gaze, "Jacob Carpenter 16" was written across the back. I had to bring him back, that or kick his ass and make him get home. "Can I keep this? I'll need whatever information you have about his friends, were he likes to hang out, and that sort of thing. He have a car? Also would I be able to see his room, check the grounds around the house? I can start right now if you'd like." I've always been one to make snap decisions, just look at my various business ventures and the drawers filled with old business cards.

Erin seemed slightly dazed by my rapid acceptance, but she was smiling. Her tears stopped and she pulled out a folded piece of paper. "I made a list of his friends already. Thank you Mr. Shaw."

"Please, it's Jon," I stood and pulled open the drawer on the right side of my desk. I carried a Kimber custom .45, everything match grade and further refined by my own hand. I slid the gun into its holster and reached for my jacket. I grabbed my car keys and came around the desk. I pulled her arm and she rose easily from the seat.

"The longer we wait the colder the trail." I gently pushed her toward the door.

"But we haven't even talked about rates, or anything, really…?"

"Believe me my rates are the lowest you'll find and I'm ready to work now." My rates were almost guaranteed to be the lowest as I hadn't even considered what they should be. Anyway, in case it's not obvious, I'm a sucker for a beautiful woman.

3

She lived in the wilds of Litchfield. It was wealthy territory with tons of sprawling houses on lots that were usually over ten acres. She was located closer to the Torrington line; the going joke was that it was the poor section of Litchfield or the rich section of Torrington.

If you were a city dweller her street would be what you would consider an ideal suburb. Nice homes lined the street, all set back with manicured front lawns, trees and shrubs forming natural barriers between the houses and ample back yards on all of them.

Her home was an older style with a full wraparound porch and a third floor. It had a detached two car garage that had been extended to the rear, low-slung, almost like a barn. There were a bunch of trees on the west side of the house, making a wall that cut them off from their neighbor on that side. The house on the other—garage—side was a nice Cape Cod in white. A small boy on a bike stared at me. I waved to him and he took off, riding into his open garage as if I had drawn my gun. I shook my head. Kids are weird sometimes.

While I surveyed the street, Erin appeared on the porch. I put a neutral expression on my face and hurried up the stairs. She couldn't have arrived more than ten minutes ahead of me but she had changed into a man's large sweatshirt. I assumed it had been her husband's, worn for comfort, as the July afternoon was warm.

The house was nice. It didn't scream wealth but everything in it was the best that could be had. The TV in the living room was a fifty inch LED. There wasn't a Wal-Mart special DVD player next to a generic home theater. Everything matched, the set-up very carefully considered. The furniture was neat, clean, practically new—though I could tell that was more from care than from actually being new. Here and there was an antique piece. Understated wealth, a very well-crafted and admirable display. It was inviting instead of a slap to the face.

For my own curiosity I let her give me a tour of the ground floor. I must admit to a certain fondness for seeing people's kitchens. It's usually the heart of a home and you can tell a lot about people from examining it. Erin's was extremely nice and boasted a smaller TV and a full rack of cookbooks, all culled from the publishing output of hosts from shows on Food TV. Someone was into the whole "celebrity chef" phenomenon.

Slightly guilty that I had delayed the case to snoop in her kitchen I gestured upward and she nodded. Her hand trailed lovingly over the massive butcher's block islanded in the centre of the room. It told me this was her sanctum and made me like her even more. It was at that point—as I followed her up the stairs and fought to keep my eyes from her rear—that I had to question my motives for rushing into the case. Sure it was my first and it was exciting that I was making this new venture work, but at the same time I knew that there was a level of lust involved in my motives. It shamed me, so I looked at her ass, because if I was going to feel guilty over it I might as well actually do it.

I think I might have been blushing when we stopped at the second floor because Erin looked at me oddly for a few seconds before gesturing to a door at the end of the hall. I tried to smile, almost certain that my face was twisting into some goofy expression that translated to, *I have gas.*

I blew out my held breath and stepped past her. I would have known the door was her son's without her guidance. It had a huge biohazard decal and DO NOT ENTER warning labels all over it. I opened the door and stepped inside, letting the door swing shut behind me, but not letting it latch.

It was a fairly large room and it was absolutely covered in stuff. Overflowing shelves filled with dust-covered LEGO models. A desk and computer laden with papers, books, magazines, and the keyboard lost somewhere in the middle. A pile of dirty clothes in one corner, a stack of amps and five guitars in the other. The room was large enough that the kid had a loveseat, 46" TV and an entire array of game consoles. I had to stop and blink, I wish my room was this cool, now or when I was his age. The walls were covered in posters, mostly of bands, many of them from the 90s or newer like My Chemical Romance, Simple Plan, Godsmack, and Bullet for my Valentine. Mixed throughout were several framed posters of older metal bands: Led Zeppelin, Iron Maiden, Black Sabbath, Krokus, Judas Priest. It was a nice collection of new and old.

I was beginning to get the idea that perhaps the late Mr. Carpenter had been involved in music. There were these old framed posters, and I saw that three of the guitars in the corner showed signs of serious usage. His leather jacket and jean vest were straight out of the late 80s.

I took a deep breath and then stepped into the center of the room. It was a jumble of *things*; every bit of shelving covered in something. Almost the entire floor was covered as well. If there was a flat bit of space anywhere it had something on it. I closed my eyes, gathered my thoughts, and then opened them and really looked at the room. Slowly turning, I surveyed every inch waiting for something to stand out in the jumble.

I noticed it halfway through my turn, but completed the full circle just in case. The window sill on the east side of the house was completely clear—also the floor beneath it; the next window over was filled with knick-knacks.

As I neared the window I noticed that there was no screen on the outside. For a moment I thought maybe this was just the window that Jacob would put his air conditioner in, but it was late July and as I glanced back toward the door I saw the control panel for central air. I opened the window and stuck my head out, it opened directly over the porch roof which was fairly flat.

I spotted a few spent cigarette butts stuck along the edges of the shingles. It looked like Jacob had a small habit. Probably liked to climb out onto the roof, maybe look at the stars and think while he smoked. Maybe ask God why his father was gone. I was veering into some heavy stuff, and I tried to clear the thoughts from my mind as I leaned back through the window.

That's when I noticed the greasepaint. I rubbed it into my fingers and pulled back into the room. It was heavy and white and after days on the windowsill it was still slightly damp. I looked at the posters and then shook my head. Not a single black metal or Goth band in sight. My Chemical Romance was pretty close to being the only pure Emo band on the wall. But not *real* black metal.

Black metal bands liked to paint their faces with masks called corpse paint, usually with white and black makeup. They were almost like trademarked logos, the way clown faces are kept in a registry. I pulled out my notebook; one of those flip-top notebooks you always see on cop shows. I quickly scrawled a couple of notes:

Liked to climb out window for smoking and/or sneaking out?

White greasepaint heavy on the outside of the window... corpse paint? Girlfriend with no taste? Why? How outside of window?

I'm 16 and pissed, where would I go?

I checked the drawers of the night stand and the desk. I found the usual teenager items: porn, a Zippo, guitar picks, notes and papers, a handful of drawings that looked like he was trying to create a band logo. I took a few of the drawings, the letters of the band names were in a gothic hooked and clawed style. Perhaps he was starting a black metal band, or even a KISS tribute. They wore the same makeup.

The KISS angle knocked me back and made more sense. I needed to get out of the room and check the porch. See if I could find a point where Jacob could have climbed down.

Erin wasn't in the hallway when I stepped out. I found her downstairs in the living room. That made me pause, *living room*. It was empty; the whole house was feeling empty. It had felt like a live place, full of warmth and joy and family. I had a premonition at that moment: I wouldn't be bringing her son back to her. This poor woman and this large house. I shivered. I suddenly understood the sweatshirt.

"I'm going to look around outside. Was your son in a band or maybe starting one up?"

"Jacob's father was a musician. Jacob inherited the talent, he was a good guitarist and he could sing as long as it was screaming or growling. The first three friends on the list I gave you are his bandmates. They haven't played all that much." The hope was still in her eyes; the more life returned to them the colder I felt. "Do you think he ran off with the band?"

I hated that sound in her voice. Hope. I was only an hour into the investigation, and I didn't want to commit to anything. "It's a possibility, I'll make that one of my avenues of investigation." I liked that line. I flipped my notebook open, wrote down the band angle and the line; *avenue of investigation*, because it sounded very professional, and grinned despite myself. It read like something you'd hear on a TV show.

I held the smile and turned it to Erin. Then I stepped outside before the moment got awkward. It already felt strained. I tried not to notice the glass in her hand or the bottle of bourbon on the table. Guilt gnawed at me despite the fact that I had done nothing wrong. I ached for this woman. Maybe I wasn't really cut out for this work. I was certain that I'd need to grow some mental calluses against this much-personal emotion, or each new case would beat me up and knock me out.

I had always imagined that my first case would be taking pictures of marital infidelity. Following some schmuck around until he went to a massage parlor and asked for a *happy ending*. Somehow I'd get the incriminating evidence. I think I was the only PI in history who actually *wanted* to follow the cheating husband and take pictures.

I walked along the side of the house looking for the open window. It was right over the driveway, and the porch ran the length of that side of the house, coming to an end at the back corner, where a side door led from the kitchen to a similar door on the extended garage. Someone had built a short roof extension so that a person could walk the couple of yards between the side of the house and the garage under cover. It also created a bridge to the garage roof. I scanned the ground along the edge of the porch and shook my head as I spotted three cigarette butts in the grass.

"Hey mister, whatcha doin?" I turned to find the boy on the

bike watching me. He was a blond-haired kid and, swear to God, was missing his two front teeth. He whistled through the gap as he eyed me warily.

"Well now, who do we have here?" I flipped open my notebook and sort of struck a pose.

"You a cop!?" The kid smiled, obviously excited by the prospect of meeting a cop.

"Private eye son and I'll be asking the questions. What's your name? I need to know if you saw anything … suspicious …on Friday night?" I don't know why, but I sort of fell into this really bad Sam Spade impression. He was more my father's favorite. It didn't matter, because I was only playing with the kid, and he seemed to enjoy it.

"I'm Tommy Mathers, sir. Live next door. You gonna arrest Jacob? He's bad; he smokes on the roof but Mrs. Carpenter doesn't know and he yells at his mom and she's a nice mom. I have a nice mom. She's pretty, you should meet her. You have a gun?" The kid was a lisping spitfire, rapid words and lots of sibilant spitting. I got lost in there for a second. I thought it was likely he had some genuine information in there. He'd heard the fight between Erin and Jacob, possibly more than one of them; he'd observed Jacob climbing out his window to smoke, and he had a pretty mom. Wait, what? Scratch that last bit.

"Slow it down son," I tried channeling my father. "Did you hear an argument on Friday?"

"Everyone heard it. They had it right here in the driveway. Jacob wanted to take his Dad's bike and his Mom said no. He said some bad words that my Mom says I'm not allowed to repeat, ever, and Mrs. Carpenter, she slapped Jacob. Right in front of the whole street. So Jacob he pushes the bike back in the garage and says something about being an adult and then he storms into the house and then my mom yelled at me to go to bed and she went out to talk to Mrs. Carpenter." Tommy grinned as he watched me frantically scrawl all that into my book.

The kid was a gold mine of information, not that knowing the cause of the fight would help all that much with discovering Jacob.

I still needed to check the edges of the porch roof for scuff marks, and now I had an idea that maybe Jacob had stolen his father's motorcycle. I walked over to the garage to peer into the window. I heard Tommy's bike as he followed me.

I put my face to the window of the garage and nearly fell through the pane. My jaw must have been on my chest and my forehead bounced off the glass before I recovered. Apparently Mr. Carpenter had been both a musician *and* a Harley-Davidson enthusiast. That garage was a mechanics dream workshop including a car lift and a bike lift. The back wall was all workbenches and tool boxes. A bare frame sat in the bike lift and right inside the door I was staring at what had to be a late 30s knucklehead chopper.

I turned and walked away from the garage, stepping around little Tommy. Unless there were more bikes in there, and I did see several shapes under tarps including a car and probably enough space left over for two more bikes, I was gonna assume that the bike in question was right inside the door because that was as far as Jacob would have pushed it before he turned and sulked back into the house.

"Ok, he didn't take the bike and he might have run off with his band… need to find those footprints or maybe a ladder…" I was talking to myself as I walked to the end of the house and porch.

Tommy didn't seem to get that. He continued my sentence. "He climbs down the back of the porch. But I don't think he joined a band. I think he ran off with the circus."

I wasn't really paying much attention to the little guy. I stepped into the back yard and noticed that they had an above ground pool with a deck built around it. From the back edge of the porch roof it was only a few feet to lower yourself to the deck railing and then down the deck steps into the back yard. I smiled and glanced back at the boy.

"You were right about him climbing down at the back of the house." Here I chuckled though. Run away to join the circus? Who says things like that anymore? I shook my head and ruffled Tommy's hair. He was a good kid.

There was some more white paint smeared on the deeply

stained wood, like maybe someone pulling themselves up using the rail, rubbing their cheek across the surface. I made a note of it and then I got down on my hands and knees and looked in the grass.

It was a bit patchy where the driveway ended, and with the porch overhang there was very little light at the edge. Most of the grass had died leaving a large area of slightly damp earth. I'm not a real tracker, but I can read some signs, including the very real, very clear depression of two large feet. At least I hoped they were feet. They were about the right size if someone was wearing shoes without tread and were really tall. I wear size thirteen boots and my print was both slimmer and shorter than the impression. I'd have to guess a triple E size fifteen dress shoe. Which was pretty much ridiculous.

The next sign didn't make me feel much better. It was a long depression that pretty much had to be someone lying on their side. I could make out a sharp divot—probably the left elbow—and just off from the depression a very clear full on handprint, right hand probably to brace and push off the ground after falling on their left side.

"TOMMY!" a woman's voice practically shrieked from nearby. It made me blink and Tommy gave a huge world weary sigh. Then he opened his mouth and yelled right back.

"WHAT? I'm talking with the detective," he sighed again and shook his head as if the other yeller was the stupidest person in the world.

I ignored the noise and concentrated on the ground. I didn't like the story it was telling me. The two huge footprints were positioned to be standing over the fallen form. Something in my heart told me the sixteen year old did not have the huge feet, but was in fact the body on the ground.

"You're with the WHAT? Where the hell are you young man!?" That would be Ms. Mathers, I assumed.

"Jeez mom, I'm right HERE. With the detective."

I shook my head and noticed something out of the corner of my eye. A glint of metal in the gravel under the deck. I reached down and picked it up. It was a *balisong*, a butterfly knife, and it was covered in the white greasepaint. I flipped the blade open with practiced ease and felt my stomach lurch; the blade was covered in more paint and blood. I heard footsteps behind me, and I slid the knife into my pocket as I stood.

A young woman came around the corner, blonde and curvy and very attractive. I wondered if I'd stepped into an alternate world where all the attractive single mothers of the world now lived. I wondered if she had a garage full of Harleys and cars to entice a guy. Of course, looking at her I didn't need a car to entice me.

The worried anger left her face and she slowed her pace, smoothing her shirt and bringing a slightly bewildered smile, crooked and very pretty, to her face.

"What's going on?" she lowered her tone.

"I told you, I'm helping the detective look for Jacob." Tommy made another long suffering sigh and rolled his eyes at me. He then rather unsubtly added, "See, I told you she's pretty."

Ms. Mathers had the good graces to pretend she didn't hear, though she did blush. "Well Tommy, it's time for dinner so get back in the house and wash up."

"But mom. I gotta help out, he needs me." Tommy turned big six-year-old eyes on me, pleading for me to intercede. Not a place I wanted to be.

"I'm sure that Detective…?"

"Shaw."

"I'm sure Detective Shaw is very grateful for the help, but it's time to get in the house. Now say goodbye. Sorry for the… whatever," She blushed again and then turned around and headed toward the house. "Five minutes and you better be in the kitchen washing your hands."

"But mom, he thought Jacob ran off with a band when he could have run away with the circus! I helped."

She glanced back, "No more, five minutes."

I think she put a little sashay in her walk and there was no way I could pass up noticing. Like I said, she was a very curvy woman.

"Ah, man. I gotta go in." Tommy said.

I knelt down so that I could meet him eye to eye and offered him my hand. He shook it and gave me another gap-toothed grin. "Let me ask you," I said, "before you go. Why do you keep bringing up the circus?"

"Cause it's right over there," Tommy pointed over my shoulder. "I gotta go. Hamburger Helper tonight, my favorite. See you later, Detective."

I watched him pedal around the garage and disappear and then turned to look over my shoulder. The Carpenter property stretched back a whole acre, maybe two as I'm not exact on the whole acre measurement thing. If I am going to keep accurate notes, I guess I needed to figure it out, but for the moment it wasn't important. I jogged across the yard. A fence made a clear line right across the yard and as I stepped up to it I felt rather foolish.

A huge field stretched for hundreds of yards beyond the fence and across the field I could make out a big top and several lesser tents in a cluster. The lights of the midway were just starting up, it was still an hour or more till dusk but I was sure people were already flocking to the tents.

I thought about the ethics of asking out Ms. Mathers and taking her boy to the circus, then ruefully shook my head. This was going to be an interesting career choice if all of the cases went like this one.

I walked back to the front of the house, pausing to take pictures of the depressions with my cell phone. I had a really nice camera. It was too bad I'd left it behind. Nice rookie mistake, but luckily I was working this alone, so no one noticed.

4

I would love to tell you that I had the whole thing solved in a matter of hours and that it was smooth sailing and all I had to do was contact his band mates and then there he was. But it wasn't that easy.

I worked through the members of the band and the rest of his friends, one after the other. The band was devastated; the bass player was an attractive girl who I immediately tagged as Jacob's girlfriend. She wouldn't admit anything with the rest of the group there, but when I got her away from them she gave me the details. The band had been started by the two of them: her brother was on the drums and a band geek had been recruited to play keyboards.

They weren't a black metal band, though they played some pretty loud and dark stuff. I figured they might be lying to me. I still held out hope that the paint and blood on the knife was from some crazy stage act. Maybe they stabbed a pig's head or something. They wouldn't be the first band to do some really revolting stuff for the shock value. The only other idea I had was perhaps a clown from the circus. I didn't really want to believe that, but knew it would have to be a focus after I finished the interviews.

It was a dead end. The hours fled as I hunted through the list of friends. Still nothing. I had one friend on the Thomaston police force. It's a small town but it supplies police to five of the neighboring townships and villages including my little corner of the state, Sentry Hill. I finished the day's interviews with a stop at the precinct house.

I gave Olaf the knife and asked him if he could tell me whether the blood was human or animal. I figured that was the most I could ask. It wasn't like they had a crime lab; and much as I might wish it, this wasn't an episode of *CSI.* We had one of the foremost experts in the world of Forensics down in New Haven—Dr. Henry Lee. But I wasn't exactly on a first name basis with him. That thought led me to consider enrolling in New Haven University and taking the Forensics Program. I shook my head. That might be a great idea for the future, but it wouldn't help me solve the current case.

It was Friday afternoon when I had finished exhausting all my leads. I had called every name on Erin's list and each one of those friends had given me more contacts to try. It was like a reverse six degrees of separation, expanding ever outward from Jacob. Hell, I even ended up calling his orthodontist.

As of that night, he'd been missing for exactly a week. I knew enough to realize that was a bad thing. The police had gotten involved mid-week, and other than walk the same ground I had already covered, they didn't seem very interested in the case. I was still waiting on word about the knife and I still had one lead to pursue.

My phone rang and I felt my bowels twist. I checked the caller ID and was relieved that it wasn't Erin. I didn't know what to tell her. Her voice over the phone had been breaking my heart. I snagged the phone out of the cradle, willing it to be good news.

"I don't have good news but it might not be bad. It just depends on your spin." The voice belonged to Edgar "Olaf" Carlsson; he was an ex-marine, a current cop, and a huge Swede. Hence the nickname. Olaf was well over six feet tall and at least two hundred and fifty pounds of muscle. He was scary as hell to see climbing out of a police car after you got pulled over.

"Look Olaf, it has to be good news, 'cause otherwise I'm stalemated." Olaf gave a light chuckle. He was a generally good natured man, just huge and scary.

"Hey JC, I can't just make stuff up just to make you happy. I only deliver the facts. The white stuff is definitely greasepaint but it's not kid's Halloween stuff. It's full-on stage makeup. We're talking Broadway and Hollywood here. Top shelf. As to the blood… 'fraid that's human, A positive."

The words hammered into me. "Christ."

"Hey careful buddy," Olaf was a devout Catholic and I actually cringed. As if he could reach through the phone and cuff me in the ear.

"Yeah sorry, but that's not really good news." I had to figure out how to ask Erin her son's blood type.

"Hey look, you got a weapon, you got blood, and you got paint that might belong to an assailant. It's pretty lean but it's enough to at least get one of the Litchfield officers looking into the case. I'd find out the kid's blood type first. Also the next time you pick up something, you might want to consider wearing gloves. Try to be a professional, JC."

"Yeah, I'm learning on the job, ok? I'm well aware of all the mistakes I'm making. I never make them twice though. Thanks again. Hey, my Dad is having a pig roast first weekend of August; bring a keg." The Swede gave a chuckle and then hung up on me.

It was pretty late and in hindsight I should have been out the door after that call. I think I had already concluded that there wasn't to be a happy ending and I wanted to push it off as long as possible. I decided to wait until morning. Who knows, maybe I would find an answer in my dreams.

I was headed towards Erin's street, trying to go over in my mind how exactly I was going to ask her about her son's blood type. All of my preplanned thoughts went out the window as I turned down the street. Half a dozen cop cars swarmed the driveways of both the Carpenter and Mathers houses. I felt sick to my stomach and I pulled over three houses down and walked to the scene.

My tension began to ease when I saw Erin standing in the yard. She had her arms around another person, wrapped in a blanket. Two officers stood nearby talking to each other.

As I got closer, Erin noticed me while the blanket wrapper person turned. It was Ms. Mathers, her face was a mask of anguish and I staggered as if gut punched. I tried to hide my discomfort but I could draw no closer to such pain.

Please tell me that Tommy is alright, I whispered to myself, but I knew that wasn't going to be the case. The cops were eyeing me and I wasn't feeling real comfortable with it. My license and business cards were in my breast pockets but I was smart enough to not reach for them.

Erin pushed Ms. Mathers—I wish Tommy had told me her name, but what six year old knows his mom's name, or tells it to someone?—to one of the cops and she threaded past another. I was surprised when she hugged me, but delighted with the contact.

"What's going on?" I felt like an idiot as I asked.

"Tommy's missing. The police think he might have been taken by his father. The divorce was a bit of a mess and Tommy's father did some time in jail. I guess he's been out for a year and last month he called saying he wanted to see him again. Poor Donna is a wreck. I mean, what's going on in this world? Two children missing in one week." She sobbed and leaned into me and I surprised even myself when I put an arm around her shoulders. She wept for a while and I just stood there, feeling helpless and angry. It was a slow simmering anger and it promised violence.

I walked Erin into her house, making sure to wend my way slowly through the knots of cops, listening in on their conversations.

"…real scumbag guy. Violent as hell, hope I run into him…"

"Kind of strange. Looks like the kid might have unlocked the door from the inside and walked out to his dad. Guess he was too young to remember Dad drunk, or beating mom…"

"… bet you the Carpenter woman is going to push *her* son's case again… shit." That officer coughing into his hand as I stepped past with Erin in my arms. Bastard.

I led her into the living room and asked if I could get her anything, but all she wanted was information about Jacob. I told her about the knife and asked her about his blood type, but I lied and told her I was still waiting for the results. I cringed when she said his blood was A Positive. I left her there, lied again and said I had to run down one more lead and that I'd be back later in the afternoon. I just wanted to clear my head, think, and maybe hope to run into Mr. Mathers and educate him on the errors of his ways.

I knew that was a fantasy, and if I beat the hell out of the man,

I would be the one in jail. I went back to my office and stood in my foyer. I had some gunsmithing work to do but I found it hard to put the case aside and concentrate on anything else. I went into my gun store and grabbed a wooden tray and a small tool box off the counter. I took both into my office and sat behind the desk. On the tray was an old cowboy shooter, a replica model that could handle modern loads and rounds. It wouldn't index properly. I knew precisely what was wrong with the piece. It was single action and cowboy quick draw guys liked to beat the hell out of their weapons. They all wanted to be Clint Eastwood and fan the hammer as fast and hard as possible, and yet still have his movie effects accuracy.

The hammer spring was a simple bar of steel. Constant battering could make them brittle and prone to breakage. It was the most likely culprit, though there was always a chance it was something in the trigger or the cylinder itself.

I flicked on the radio and started taking apart the weapon, humming along to the music as I removed the cylinder—it looked pretty good—and then the handle so I could get to the back strap. As soon as the grips came off, the weakened spring fell apart. I felt a surge of satisfaction that I'd been right. It was great to have something go right.

I think God prefers me unhappy. The music went off the radio, replaced by the local DJs talking about events. I sighed and once again considered getting a satellite radio or just turning on my computer. Then I paid attention.

"... yesterday was the last day for the circus in Litchfield. Did you get a chance to see it Bobby? It was a real class act, totally unique mixture of American and European..."

I had wanted to take Tommy to the circus, but I had never gone back because I was avoiding Erin. Now he couldn't see the circus.

Couldn't see the circus?

It hit me then and I knew I truly was a huge idiot. White greasepaint. I had ignored that line of reasoning, had focused on the friends and peers of Jacob. Tommy said that Jacob had run off with the circus. What if he wasn't guessing? What if he had actually seen Jacob head to the circus? Or what if a pedophile dressed as a clown had been peeking on Jacob?

The scenario played out in my mind's eye. The rebellious teen in his room, angry at everything. He turns and notices a clown staring into his window. I shook my head to clear the image of a clown in full makeup. Perhaps it was a clown that was still mostly made up, like just off shift. Do clowns and carnies have shifts? I digress. I can imagine Jacob going after the peeker. Chasing the clown to the edge of the roof where he drops off, creating the two large footprints in the damp earth.

I can see Jacob slowing at the edge and starting to climb down and the clown reaching up, yanking his arm and dropping him onto his side. Jacob pulls out his knife, the two struggle, and the clown ends up with the knife. He cuts Jacob.

I can see the clown taking the boy over the fence and across the field. Carnies stick together, they help hide the boy, then they do terrible things to the boy.

I could no longer concentrate on fixing the gun. I stood, hands trembling and my chair rolling across the room. I had made notes to check the circus and I had ignored them. It had seemed so unlikely, so farfetched, and yet my gut was telling me it was so right. The images came faster. The pedophile coming again to take a younger boy, one with less fight. I saw red for a while. My senses were awash with emotions, chief among them shame and guilt.

I wasn't thinking too clearly or perhaps I was deluding myself, in hindsight I know exactly what was going through my mind. I pulled open the drawers of my desk and pulled out my gun and a backup piece. The Kimber went into my shoulder holster and a subcompact Glock found its way to my ankle. I headed for the door.

5

I crossed the field and resisted the urge to draw one of my pistols. First off, I was already on private property, and secondly I was going to an empty area. Who would I shoot?

The circus was long gone. I passed from the knee-high grass into a wide open area. It was as if I'd stepped through some invisible barrier. A tingle ran down my spine as I stepped onto an area of dirt and flattened plants. I tried to ignore my imagination, but even though I was in the middle of a clear field, under bright sunshine, I could have sworn that it was at least twenty degrees cooler.

I stretched and loosened my stiff limbs and shook the sudden chill out of my legs. The sudden image of Tommy's toothless smile spurred the anger in my belly and I got to work.

Most of what I do is really just *seeing* and *listening*; in other words, paying attention to the world around me. I turned a slow circle and tried to imagine the layout of the tents. The Big Top would have been to the back and center of the area with the midway leading up to it. It was the best way to draw the crowd through the food carts, games, and other attractions and make them spend money before they entered.

The place was strewn with garbage and it didn't take much of a detective to determine that all the food stalls had been lined up along an area that was gravel and dirt. They'd been placed as far away from the dry grass as possible. I found spots where grease had been illegally dumped, the gravel stained black by the oils.

I wandered along my imaginary midway looking at the discarded cigarette butts, sticks that might have held grilled steak or corndogs, tons of fallen popcorn that was attracting no end of birds, and other refuse. I think that was when the chills returned.

I had noticed the birds as I crossed the field but I just realized then that I hadn't heard a sound out of them since I had left the grass. All around me crows hopped along, snagging dropped kernels of corn, their heads tilting to the sides so that they could keep a glassy eye on me. It was damn strange. Crows are noisy birds, always yelling at you like a rude construction worker whistling as women pass by. Stereotypes, yeah, but based on fact. Crows are never quiet.

I shivered and watched the birds watching me. I bet if I'd fired a round, they'd all have scattered. I contained the urge and continued my walk. I ignored the strange crows until one of them took to the air with a sharp flap of wings. It broke the silence and it startled me. A bunch of feathers drifted to the ground and lit on a forgotten stuffed bear. It was a little worse for wear, one ear torn off leaving a tear down the side of its face. It was just lying there with a flyer trapped under its feet.

I pushed the bear away, snatched up the flyer and resisted the urge to wipe my hand on my pants.

"Christ," I told myself, "get a hold of yourself. It's just a toy that got lost or some carnie threw away."

At the sound of my voice dozens of crows took to the air. As they flew they shrieked and cried. Hearing them break their silence, I actually felt relieved. They circled above me, waiting for me to go away or at least get far enough that they could return to their feast.

I jogged over to the area I had mentally mapped as the main tent, then I looked at the sheet of paper in my hands. It was a standard flyer printed on legal size paper. It was nothing fancy; I could have whipped it up on my computer in a matter of minutes.

It read: HENRY HOLMES CIRCUS. A EUROPEAN DELIGHT.

It was covered in poorly scanned photos, along with a few stylized drawings. Most of the images showed an array of men and women in various states of undress, covered in tattoos and piercings and performing the basics of an old-time vaudeville show. They had a fire eating team, a Geek—that's someone who can eat anything and not a *nerd*—covered in a jigsaw tattoo, several contortionists, and strongmen—all the basics of the old days of Circus.

"They look like a bunch of self-made freaks." It was the second time I'd spoken out loud to myself. It made me feel better to hear my own voice. For the first time I wished I had a partner, though that would have dulled the romantic notions I had of the job.

Speaking of freaks, and I don't use the term in a derogatory manner, the word was splashed across the bottom half of the paper. The Holmes Circus had two other draws beside their Big Top of "Death Defying Stunts." One was a separate tent containing one of the world's last remaining "Traveling Freak Shows." I couldn't be sure, but I would have sworn that actual "freak shows" had been outlawed decades ago. It wasn't really an area of the law I was familiar with and probably not germane to the case. To be fair, there are few areas of the law I'm really familiar with, and I just like the way the word "germane" sounds. Sue me.

The last attraction caught my attention: European versus American Clowning. The picture at the bottom of the flyer was literally some sort of slapstick melee brawl. The photos were black and white and grainy, but I stared at the images of the clowns, wondering which one of them was the bastard I would have to hunt down. I was so certain of my theory that I was getting sick from adrenaline.

As if a clown would suddenly appear in the grass and shout that I'd found him. I'd put off training for the week and I needed to burn off some energy before I lost my temper and did something I'd regret. There was nothing more that I wanted at that moment than to have a half-dozen students rush me so that I could toss them all over the mats. My hands shook. The students didn't deserve that and my Sensei would be angry with me if I took my aggression out on her class. I took a deep breath and wondered if there were any *shit kicker bars* in the area. Wouldn't take much to walk in, say "Country music sucks," and get a brawl going.

The image inspired me to laugh and my tension eased. The adrenaline bled off and left me shaky. I cracked my neck, easing the tension, and walked through the area that had housed the main tent.

I folded the poster and placed it in my back pocket. I had a pair of surgical gloves stuffed in there and removed them. Olaf had been right in chiding me and I donned the gloves. Just in case I found something.

The circus boasted European roots and I wondered if it contained actual gypsies. I found an area beyond the tent and the back perimeter of the circus ground that must have been a campground. Beside the fact that it had numerous wheel ruts from trucks and trailers, it had no less than a dozen fire pits arranged in a circular pattern. A mostly circular pattern, there was one large pit that was over a hundred feet back from the rest.

I wandered from pit to pit. Most of them were just cold coals over stone beds. These guys knew how to build a safe fire and they had been careful to put them out completely. I guess not everyone involved with the circus was bad. I knew I couldn't assume the whole circus was behind the disappearances, though I was leaning toward believing that the clown hadn't acted alone. You'd have to be damn strong to lift a large teenage boy over an eight foot fence.

The last pit was all the way at the back of the camp. It was actually dug down into the earth, a real pit. From the debris around the edges, it looked like it had been meant solely for refuse.

I searched around and came up with a broken tent stake. It was nearly three feet long and as thick around as my wrist. The one end was smooth from all the times it had been hammered into the earth.

I started sifting through the coal and ash at the bottom of the pit, pushing aside lengths of charcoal and less identifiable lumps. One looked like it might have been a waxed paper cup, another looked like an empty condom foil, and still another might have been a melted spork.

I didn't know what I expected to find. I seriously doubted I would dig down and uncover a leering skull, and yet every time I pushed the ashes aside, that was exactly what I expected.

I reached the stone-lined bottom and sighed. It was more of nothing. I widened the hole in the ash and found two lumps of metal. I threw the stake aside and reached into the pit. There was still some residual warmth in the stones and I picked up the black lumps. I rubbed them in my palm and a bright sheen was revealed. Silver?

I dove into the ashes with my gloved hands, scooping away ashes and shoving them hurriedly to the edge of the pit. My jacket was soon covered in pale ash and a cloud above me clearly marked that I was trespassing on private property. I didn't care.

I found a skull. Thankfully not the one I feared to find, but it was just as damning. It was a silver skull and crossbones, the edges of the bones having melted from the heat, along with the other two lumps I'd already found. I was certain that these three pieces were what remained of the piercings that had adorned Jacob Carpenter's face.

6

As much as I love movies and I reference them for my own behavior on the job, I've never actually believed everything I've seen in them. I've never believed in cops that are apathetic or would actually rather eat a donut instead of doing their jobs. I knew Olaf and the handful of guys had pulled me over because the pipes on my bike were too loud, or I was going too fast, or looked too young, or for whatever reason. Most of them were doing their jobs, and yeah, some of them were just out to bust your balls. They still did their jobs.

I sat in the precinct, face red and hands shaking; while an equally red faced officer yelled back at me that I was wrong and very close to "pushing my luck." I didn't know what type of threat that was supposed to be, but I was calculating in my mind just how long I'd be in jail if I knocked this guy out and asked for a decent cop instead. The fact that a handful of other officers were scattered around the room watching this also had me leery. The Chief was out, making a public appearance to show how important the Mathers kidnapping was, and I was left with the Desk Sergeant.

"Look Sarge," I said, and he bristled when I used the familiar nickname. I pointed at the sandwich bag with the lumps of silver in it. "This is at the very least enough evidence to change the Carpenter *runaway* into a kidnapping, even if you're unwilling to admit that it's a sign of foul play." My voice was rising and I tried to control it. Two of the other officers in the room moved closer, one of them sat on the edge of a desk next to me. He tried to smile reassuringly as he sipped at a cup of coffee.

"Hoo ho, another kidnapping. *Foul Play*. Look Private *Dick*, I'm glad you make money playing cop but lemme tell you, these lumps don't tell me shit. Mebbe kid actually runs off with the circus, who knows. We got a real deal kidnapping to deal with."

He tossed the baggie from hand to hand as he talked and then threw it against my chest. I caught it and took a deep breath. Coffee cup hid a look of distaste behind his mug. It helped calm me; I might have a friend here after all.

"Let me tell you all the things wrong with what you just said, ignoring the grammar." Coffee cup snorted into his mug and Sarge, whose name was Harriman, flushed a deeper shade of red. His balding head looked hot enough to fry an egg on. "First off if he *had* run off to the Circus, then why would he have done it a week before they left? Why not run away the night they pull up stakes? Second, why would he throw away over an ounce of pure silver? It would have been better to sell it for the cash he'd need on the road. Third, you have two young boys both disappear inside of a week, both are neighbors and a circus just happens to be in their back yard. A circus that pulls up stakes and leaves the very morning Tommy Mathers goes missing? Do I need to draw a fucking map to the conclusion?"

Maybe swearing had been too much. Harriman stood up far faster than I would have given him credit. Both of his fists smashed into the top of his desk, and a pen went flying. I eased back from the desk, nearly tripping over my chair, and coffee cop was at my shoulder, a hand on my bicep in a friendly but firm grip.

"Lemme tell you something, you punk. I been busting my ass for longer than you've been alive. You think I'm no cop 'cause I shine this chair with my ass and coordinate these guys? You're wrong. You make some points but lemme tell you about this boy Jacob Carpenter. He's trouble. He's spent time in juvie already and has a list of crimes that are only going to grow into a career criminal's jacket. We have theft, disturbing the peace, destruction of private property, vandalism and, get this one, armed assault. Your boy likes to fight. So mebbe he takes on some of these gypos you got a hard-on for and he bets the jewelry. How they end up in a fire who knows, who cares. You bring me some bloody clothes or a body the next time you want to cry murder."

Harriman eased back from his desk, took a deep breath and eyed the mess he'd created on his desk. He continued, "As to Tommy, that's a damn shame and I'll tell you this, his scumbag father took him. Yeah, you know his father was a criminal? Huh *Private Dick*? Yeah we wanted him on a bunch of crimes but the only one we could get to stick was beating his wife. She tased his ass and bundled him up like a present for us. Cheshire Prison is overcrowded and the bastard has been a good little boy, no priors, so they let him go. He hasn't showed up for his parole for a month and now his boy is missing. One plus one equals two, buddy. I don't know how you do your thing but we take the clearest straightest route." He nodded to the cop behind me and the pressure on my arm was increased. I was pulled away from the desk.

"Well for your sake I hope you're right, 'cause if the circus took the boy we'll never see him again."

Harriman sighed, and his voice followed me out of the room, "I hope I'm right too."

He was a bastard but somewhere inside the man had been a good cop. The other cop, coffee cop, eased his grip as we hit the lobby.

"Sorry about Sarge. He has some issues and hasn't been the same… well, never mind. You have a card?" I appraised the cop. He was younger than me and looked like he had been listening to my words.

I opened my coat and pulled out my business card, taking a quick glance to make sure it wasn't an old one. I glanced above his badge—Bruen. "Thanks for listening officer. I have to go tell my client that her son might be dead."

He flinched. I didn't mean to push any of my anger onto him. Hell I wasn't even mad at Harriman anymore. All my rage was focusing on the circus.

"It's a tough thing to do. What are you planning to do?"

I hadn't expected the question, especially from a cop, and I had to carefully consider my words. "I'm gonna go after the circus and see if Jacob Carpenter is a carnie."

He nodded and glanced at my empty holster, I let my coat fall across it and turned on my heel and headed for the door.

"Good hunting," he called after me.

Good hunting indeed. I had no idea what I was going to do or where to begin. I needed to talk to Erin and needed to know more about the circus. I decided to do the research first; I wanted to put off the talk for as long as possible.

7

I am not a master of Internet searching. You want your computer repaired or your whole house networked, I got you covered. You want some basic cleanup on your website, some simple graphics and such; I can whip up the programming. Not that I write code straight from my head, but I know enough to fake it and I know the places to get it then copy and paste.

My Google-Fu, however, was weak. I managed to turn up several hits on HENRY HOLMES CIRCUS. Most of it was rave reviews about the clown war and *European Chic*. Whatever the hell that meant. It was likened to a cross between Cirque du Soleil and the Jim Rose Sideshow with the bonus of kiddy rides. Most of the reviews were from European websites lending credence to origin of the troupe.

For a few moments I actually found myself wanting to go as a customer. I only had to look at the lumps of silver in the baggie to pop back to reality. My search also pulled up an entirely different Henry Holmes. It wasn't a pleasant string of links. America's unofficial first serial killer was one Doctor H. H. Holmes. I wondered if the name was deliberate or if a modern man with the same name had simply started a circus. I went with the former, my anger had me marking the entire circus as a front for criminal deeds and I found myself cursing everyone involved with the act.

I found a blog supposedly belonging to one of the members of the troupe, a contortionist named Skylar Monroe. I clicked on the link and was shocked by the image that appeared. Skylar was a very attractive girl with short green hair and eyes of the same brilliant hue. She was also completely nude and curled into a tight knot that didn't look humanly possible.

I will admit to lingering over the site for a while. It's not like it was a pure porn site. All of the pictures were "artistic" and the bulk of the site was her journal. Besides finding a store that sold archival prints of all her pictures, I also happened upon a partial itinerary for her appearances for the next six weeks.

After Litchfield, Connecticut, they were moving on to Poughkeepsie, New York. That was all the information I needed. If I was Jacob Carpenter, I might have considered running off with this girl. It still didn't dismiss my fears or anger.

I pulled out a sheet of paper and started making a list. It was a habit of mine that helped me to focus. I listed the tasks that needed doing and listed the items I would need to get each job done, depending on how the scenario unfolded. I wished I had been able to get some MILSPEC night-vision goggles. My father had a pair, but refused to let me have them and wouldn't buy another pair for me.

Focus.

What I didn't know and wouldn't learn until much later was that my search had not gone unnoticed. Several of my keyword choices had triggered a series of alerts. They were extremely subtle and only executed their function when the number of keywords hit a certain number or combination.

I hit the magic number pretty quickly. An alarm went off on a computer hidden in a bunker underneath the Arizona sands. A man I've yet to meet face to face went to work and very quickly captured all of my search results, copied every link I opened, and made notes of the ones I'd yet to open. A few deft keystrokes and he let the computer do its job while he started a file on me, hacked into the DMV and other Federal agencies to dump every bit of public and private information about my life into a computer file folder, and at the same time composed emails to other members of his network. The emails would be held until I triggered one deeper level alert in his system.

Despite that great flurry of activity, I had only tripped the warning bell.

I, of course, was oblivious to all of this. I merely saved a few pictures for future investigative purposes and then printed the address for the next show location.

8

The task at the top of my list was the hardest one to perform.

I pulled into Erin's driveway and approached the door. The cop and media circus had departed and—considering I didn't know how things would go in New York—I needed to see Erin to prepare her for the worst.

I was sick to my stomach as I waited for the door to open. As it swung wide I steeled myself. Something in my expression must have given me away. The light left her eyes, the final spark of hope faded. I felt like shit and I hadn't even opened my mouth.

I stepped into the house and took her into my arms. She punched me in the chest a few times, each blow weakening until I was the only thing keeping her on her feet. I carried her into the living room and put her on the couch. She got hold of herself quickly.

"Tell me everything. I need to know." Her voice was surprisingly cool, though the anguish was still in her eyes. I had to admire the strength of this woman.

"It's not a hundred percent. Believe me, the Litchfield PD took me down a peg and let me know exactly how much they didn't like my ideas," I began.

"The bastards, was it Sergeant Harriman?"

"Yeah, actually it was." The pain in her eyes gave way to the glint of anger.

"I'm not surprised. We have previous issues with Harriman. Jacob took his patrol car and parked it at the precinct house with empty beer bottles, condoms, and donut boxes filling the seats. Harriman didn't see the humor in it." A smile attempted to appear but her pain and anger crushed it.

I chuckled and pushed on. I pulled out the baggie with the

lumps of silver and she lost her control again. I've said it before but I'll say it again: I CAN'T STAND TO SEE A WOMAN CRY. My hands shook and I had to grind my teeth to stop the wrong words from tumbling out.

Erin's control inspired me and I continued. "Look, it's not a sure thing that anything bad has happened to him. Maybe he's with the circus, maybe had a fight, I really don't know for sure, at least not based on this little bit of evidence. I do believe my gut, though, and if you're ready I'll tell you what they're telling me."

She nodded, her eyes dry again.

"I think a clown had something to do with it. Maybe a Peeping Tom," I decided to keep the pedophile thing to myself, though I would have to think of some way to work out the end of my theory. "This peeper came to the house and was climbing on your porch roof looking to get a view... he finds Jacob's room not yours. Jacob sees this guy still mostly in his clown makeup and hauls off after him. They shuffle and Jacob falls, probably hurts himself. He draws a knife on this clown, the two of them fight over it and things don't go well."

She was ashen and I stopped. I knew I had to tell her the rest, but I couldn't go on. Then I realized my error earlier in the day. I had never told the cops about the damn butterfly knife and Jacob's blood type all over it. What a god damn rookie mistake. I grimaced, then she reached out and grabbed my hand.

"Please... go on and tell it all. Don't give me the half-truth version, just say it all." Damn strong woman.

"I found a knife under your deck and it was covered in greasepaint and human blood. Type A Positive. So following my hunch, I see Jacob hurt and trying to stab the clown and the clown grabbing the knife, possibly wresting it from his grasp and cutting the boy. There was no blood on the ground, so it couldn't have been a deep cut or stabbing. Now the Peeping Tom has two crimes and he panics... or he's cold enough to seize the moment. He grabs your son and drags him across the field, or more likely gets him to his feet and force walks him to the fence.

"Tommy Mathers sees Jacob and the clown walking together

and the circus in the field. He thinks Jacob is running off with the clown to join the circus. It's all just fun and games to a six year old; he doesn't realize he's seeing a kidnapping. Now if Jacob is walking, then the clown forces him to climb the fence and things proceed however they proceed. If Jacob is not walking, then the clown has help lifting your boy over the fence and it muddies things."

I preferred the version with the clown making Jacob climb over the fence. I should have checked the fence for blood or grease-paint—another mistake.

"Now, my gut tells me something bad happened to Jacob. I don't have any solid proof, but that's what I'm thinking. I also think the clown came back and took Tommy." Erin flinched like I'd slapped her. I pushed on. "I believe that the clown came back and Tommy saw him. He wanted to go to the circus; hell, he asked me to take him. He really wanted to go and seeing a clown in the yard, he wouldn't have had an issue with opening the door and letting the man in or running out to him. That's why the door was unlocked."

She shook her head, trying to dismiss my words, but I saw them taking root. The image of the small boy, delight in his eyes as he opened the door to the clown. A single tear rolled out of her right eye and tracked across her cheek. When I'd met her a week earlier, I had thought her a few years younger than me. The grief had brought her right to her natural age.

"You're telling me that some pervert clown assaulted my son and then days later came back and stole a second child? What about Ronald?"

I blinked, I didn't know the name but I quickly reasoned that she meant Tommy's father. "I think he's just an easy target. He jumped parole but that doesn't make him a kidnapper. Look, the cops have blown me off, and I'm pretty much at a stalemate. I can't honestly take any more of your money. What I would like though is your permission. I know where the circus is going and I want to go after them. I want to find this clown and have some words with him. Maybe I can get one or both of the boys back, if I'm fast enough."

"Permission?" She looked confused and then her eyes flicked down to my open jacket and exposed gun. "You want my permission to"—eyes on the gun—"save Tommy? You think it's too late for Jacob but you want to save Tommy?" She blinked more tears. Her expression steeled, eyes hard points in a mask of grief. "Get Tommy and get that bastard clown."

It was all I needed to hear. I had a focus for my anger. The only question remaining was…which clown was the monster?

During the few-hour drive to Poughkeepsie, I had time to formulate a plan. Well, to be honest, I had time to think up dozens of ideas, half of which were so stupid I refuse to put them into print here. Then again, considering the outcome of the plan I settled on, I guess it's subjective which plan was really the dumbest.

I knew I was going to drive around the area at least a few times. Scout all the ways to and from and try to have a plan of escape. Exit strategy was top of my list. Especially since almost every plan had me breaking multiple laws. I was licensed to carry a firearm in New York but going armed into a camp where I might have to break into a private camper and defend myself against carnies and a pedophile clown was a different story. Yeah, trespassing, assault, assault with a deadly weapon, breaking and entering, stalking, and maybe manslaughter if things got out of hand. Sure, most or all of those charges would drop if I found Tommy or Jacob, but if I was wrong I'd be in jail.

I will admit in hindsight that my plan was more than just foolish; it was outright dangerous. I drove through the streets of Poughkeepsie, watching the blip on my GPS and I got confused. I was right in the middle of everything, not that the town was a metropolis, but I was in the middle of a shopping district. Four-lane wide roads with all the shopping you could imagine running down either side of the roadway, and yet that was where the thing was guiding me.

I finally arrived at the area that was supposed to be housing the circus, at least per Skylar Monroe's website. It was a huge paved parking lot, an auxiliary parking area to a large strip mall. There was a small field in the back half of the lot and there was some activity there.

It was a public parking area and more than a dozen cars and SUVs were already parked in the area, despite the fact that the nearest edge of the strip mall was almost a third of a mile away. I wondered if this place ever did enough business to actually fill the regular lot, let alone need this extra area. I stepped out of my car and grabbed my camera, I had a character disguise all in mind for this and looking over the area I figured that I might have a little help in that department.

There were several people I took to be locals, mostly just curious gawkers who had come out to see the circus. Of the circus I didn't see much, and I was worried. There were several battered trucks, one camper and a semi truck with a fifty-two foot trailer. The trailer was being offloaded by a score of burly men. It looked like the main tent and lighting systems.

That was all that was present. I knew there were two more tents and an entire midway of food stalls, game stalls, and more than twenty rides. Where the hell was the rest of the troupe? I fought down the worry and decided to move into the area. I needed to get into character.

As I got closer I could make out more details. There were indeed a bunch of local folks looking at the set up. A handful of them were burly men who looked like they were out of work. They were more interested in the offloading and set up of equipment and whether they could work it into a few hours of employment. The rest were just there to see the attractions and get a feel for what would be going on at the circus. I saw one other person with a camera and for a second I panicked, thinking they were going to blow the cover I'd created. I was coming in as Mitch *Nolastname* a blogger/cameraman for *Tri-State Color,* a blog about attractions and events throughout the New York, New Jersey, and Connecticut area. The other cameraman was probably part of the local news paper or something similar. I gave him a wide berth and boldly walked closer.

I pulled up the camera to obscure my face and began to snap random shots as I watched the activity. The movers were all large men, but in the middle of them was a bearded giant standing at least six and a half feet tall. He was a solid barrel of a man, thick in both the stomach and chest area, solid rather than chiseled. I had to guess him at three hundred or more pounds and capable of throwing a keg over each shoulder with ease.

Based on his build and size I thought I could handle him, as long as he didn't have any training I didn't know about. It was still a scary thought and I needed to file it away, especially if I was going to return tonight and move through the camp. Then again, there appeared to *be* no camp.

I snapped some pictures of the men working. The giant appeared to be in charge, or at the least he was a second-in-command. I did see him defer to one man a few times but could never catch that one's face. The giant noticed me; he turned his large, bearded face my way and I snapped off a picture. In the picture screen his eyes were hooded, mean looking and small under a heavy brow, and the entire bottom half of his face was obscured in at least a year's growth of thick, black beard, but I could still make out a frown.

"You shouldn't be takings their pictures, is very rude you know," it was a thick accent, but comprehensible, and in my head a flag waved as Hungarian or Austrian. Not that I was particularly good with accents. *Takingez... pict-Zorz*, a lot of Z sounds in there.

"Ah well, excuse me then, I mean no disrespect. I was hoping to catch some of the acts," I turned to find a very *compact* man. Compact was the best word I could use for him, he was neat and small, but well proportioned for his size. He was maybe five and a half feet tall, but his shoulders were broad. He wore a very expensive handmade suit, tailored exactly to his frame. I wanted the name of his tailor. He had a certain Victorian flair: heavy brocade coat, knotted and pinned cravat, silk waist coats, matching pants, and polished shoes. I was willing to bet he had a watch on a fob chain tucked into his waist coats. Perched on his nose where those glasses, *pince-nez* I believe, the ones with no arms.

He was pale, eastern European, with dark hair just touched with grey and an intricately waxed mustache that curled around his mouth. His eyes were gray and they looked like they could be hard eyes, mean, though currently he seemed either amused or curious. I wanted his picture.

I realized I had lost my train of thought, "Forgive me, my mind wandered. I'm Mitch and I'm doing a blog on this circus for Tri-State Color dot com. We cover attractions and events in the area." I shoved my hand toward him to be shaken. His grip was firm and he gave me exactly three shakes before he let go.

"Ahhh, modern technology assisting my small troupe. Well Mitch, you are very early if you're looking to 'see any of the acts'. We don't open until next weekend and this is merely a preliminary. We measure the tent and figure out the best set-up. My circus is always in harmony with the location."

Part of me wishes I could remember his accent to write it out perfectly, but the dialect doesn't look good on the page, nor does it make for easy reading. The best I can think of is a lot of Bela Lugosi with a bit of a modern dash. *Vell Mitch….*

He was subtle, but with a little pressure on my arm and a few steps, he'd led me deeper into the area that would be the heart of the circus. I was far from the locals, and also alone with this strange man.

"Ah! Forgiveness, I have visited you with rudeness. See act begets act. I am Henry Holmes, Ringmaster of the Cirque. Or at least the English version of my name, you don't have to print that part, but Henrik is too…German for the show, yea?" He stepped away from me and spun around with his arms wide. It was a rapid motion and obviously he reveled in showmanship. I gestured to the camera and he nodded, instantly offering a posed shot. I took the picture.

"Now as I was sayings, you are here too early for the big picture. But you must imagine. Here we are standing in the mouth of the great tent. The ring in the center and all the peoples will be around in the stands. The show is glorious time. Acts of old with acts of new very much presence in the ring." He turned back to me and turned me around; we stepped out of his imaginary tent. He tried to put his arm around my shoulder but I was nearly a foot taller than him so he settled for a hand in the middle of my back. I tried to edge away, not because of the contact, but from fear that he would slide his arm around my ribs to my side and feel my gun.

"Now, keeping the imagining you must to see the lane filled with the lights and the food and games. The happy children and our very fair games. No rigged games in my circus, I swear on my blood. Happy Children." He let me go and did another little pirouette dance down his imaginary midway. I couldn't help but smile. I was so confused. This man seemed like a great person, genuinely in love with the circus, and with his show. How could he harbor the monster I was looking for? I shook my head to clear the conflicting thoughts and dismiss his fantasy. Before me was little more than a parking lot with a bunch of taped-down power cables and several swarthy men setting up equipment and marking out areas for the stalls.

"Yes, yes, I can see the midway and the other two tents and all the rides. I can imagine it all. But what about the camp and the people? When will they get here?" I realized that my tone might have been a little sharp and something flickered across his face. Had I noticed his eyes narrowing? His smile had definitely eased a bit. "What I mean to say is, when will the rest of the acts be arriving? I would certainly love to get pictures of the actual tents. The internet is a visual medium and people won't flock to an empty lot with a caption telling them to imagine."

I don't think it was really a good save but Henry seemed to relax just the same. "Well *Mitch*, we have just arrived in the city today. My people need to set up their camp and I always give them a day or two of rest. I am not a taskmaster, just a ringmaster," he chuckled at his own joke, and then grinned, "Perhaps if you came here on Wednesday we would be more accommodating. I could get some good photo setup for you. Maybe an interview with some of my best peoples?"

He was sweetening the pot; either he really liked to play the media or just loved the general attention. The giant walked up to Henry and I cringed. Up close the man was scary as hell. His skin was a sallow, waxy hue. For a second I almost thought his cheeks and forehead—the only areas not covered by thick black hair—were actually crafted from wax. The few teeth that appeared in his beard-covered mouth were rotten and crooked and I could only imagine how foul his breath had to be. He leaned down and whispered something to Henry and I feigned nonchalance as I tried to hear his words. It wasn't worth the effort, the huge man was talking in rapid-fire Hungarian, at least that was the way I was leaning. I knew German and Spanish—and by default some French and Italian as they have a similar Latin root. I didn't recognize the words, but I did remember from my language classes my teacher talking about how Hungarian has a strange root, the Magyar language, which wasn't an Indo-European base.

I stood there with a smile on my face and tried to hide the worry as they continued their rapid fire conversation. Henry was speaking clearly and forcefully and the giant kept looking at me as he rumbled out his words. His voice had a deep burr to it, almost like something was vibrating in his chest as he spoke. His eyes bothered me and I fiddled with my camera to give me something else to look at.

"Lazlo! Enough, get back to your work, I need to finish with Mitch." Henry held a single hand up to Lazlo and the giant bowed his head. He lumbered away without a backward glance and I was glad. "Well, as you can see, we have very much going on right now. I can understand getting the jump on your… blog… but I'm afraid this will have to be ending. It was pleasure showing you around what little is ready. You will be returning? Come for story but also come for show?" He opened his coat and I saw the pocket watch on its silver chain. I repressed a smile as he reached into his pocket and pulled out a handful of tickets. He shoved them into my palm and shook my hand—again three pumps only.

"Now forgiveness, but I must see to the work and the camp." He smiled and gave a slight bow, a bend at the hips and then he stood straight. He gestured, a grand sweep of his arm that clearly indicated I needed to move the heck out. I took off, but as I went, I glanced back; he watched me go for a few seconds and then walked over to his workers.

The gawkers had mostly dispersed and I walked toward my car wondering how I was going to find their camp. It was late in the afternoon, well after five and I didn't know how the public buildings worked here, but back home I wouldn't be able to walk into City Hall and get my hands on camping records at this hour. I could try asking the locals, maybe look for a diner and see if any of the drivers or movers had come in looking for food. A whole convoy of trailers and semi trucks had to make some kind of impression. I was sitting on my hood thinking it through when luck smiled upon me.

A battered 40s pickup truck rolled across the parking lot and parked near the trailer. All of the workers perked up and started heading for it. I watched as two women jumped out of the cab with waves and smiles. They lowered the tailgate and began pulling large aluminum trays. It looked like dinner had arrived.

I pulled out my laptop and opened it on the hood of my car. I made it look like I was typing, but in reality I was merely waiting for the truck to depart. If I had it figured right, it would lead me back to the camp.

I made a show of ignoring the workers and tried to refine my plan. It would work better if I tried it earlier in the evening. Lazlo and his gang were all big men; if I infiltrated the camp while they were still here working, maybe I could get to the clown without much trouble.

The truck was getting ready to go. I climbed into my car and took a quick glance at myself in the rear-view mirror. The face looking back at me seemed to be accusing me of being crazy, and I had to agree with it.

The pickup took off and I slowly followed it out of the lot. I was so intent on not losing my quarry that I didn't notice the van that pulled in behind me.

9

The camp was only a few miles away, tucked off the main road. When the GPS indicated the turn-off, I continued for another mile. There was a diner off to the side of the road, and I decided it was time for my dinner.

I had breakfast for dinner. I like nothing better than having a massive plate of eggs and hash browns and hash and a side of bacon. You may get the idea that I sometimes like to binge. I finished the food and then relaxed, easing back to drink my third cup of coffee.

I figured I had two ways into the camp: one, I could walk in and pretend to be a Skylar stalker, pretend I was there trying to meet the sexy contortionist, just an over eager fan. Most likely they would only run me off and it would be no big deal, especially as I didn't intend to run into the girl. No harm to her in this plan, and they *probably* wouldn't harm me. Second; I could go in bold, make a fuss and holler about how I wanted a certain clown, that I knew things, and cause enough of a ruckus that the clown would hear about it. Maybe I could draw him out.

Yeah—I know. As I sat there mulling it over, it didn't sound good to me either. Both plans kind of sucked and in the long run I decided to wing it. Maybe do a little mix and mash. Hell, I could even play up being Mitch and say that Henry Holmes had sent me to the camp to do interviews. He was still overseeing the raising of the tent. If I got there early enough, no one would be able to find him.

I left money on the table and headed back to the car. I pulled out my GPS and plotted an alternate route to the campground. I wanted to arrive on the other side, or at least from a different road than the one used by the circus. If the place was large enough they should have several entrances. I lucked out and found one that was only a few miles away.

I parked my car in an area set up for what my dad would call "soft camping." It was filled with cabins, the parking lot secluded by a wall of trees and the outside world blocked off by acres of woods in every direction. It had running water, heat, electricity, and it was only a matter of a few minutes of walking to hit a major road and civilization.

I found a map of the grounds and figured out where the circus had set up. There were only two areas that catered to trailers and only one of those opened onto the road the pickup truck had taken. I made a sketch of the area on a sheet of paper and mapped the route in my mind as best I could. I would have to go through about a half mile of woods before I hit a huge valley of rolling grass and the trailer park.

I jogged through the trees and wondered if I was crazy. My anger was abated by the fear pumping through my veins. I will admit I've done some reckless things in my time. I speed occasionally but, for the most part, I'm a fairly law abiding man. Here I wanted to do what was right for once, and the law was likely to label me the bad guy if things went even slightly south.

I got turned around in the trees but eventually stumbled into the grassy embankment stretching down to the camp. I could make out several single trailers and RVs lined up on one end of the valley, while on the other was a veritable town of them. I took off down the hill with more speed than stealth. This was mostly public land so I had no fear of being spotted; I was more worried about getting into the inner camp. That land was paid for and until the contract was up, it basically belonged to the circus.

It was surprisingly easy to get into the camp. Not many people were out and the trailers were parked in such a way that they gave me plenty of cover. There were several canvas tents as well, and there was a bonfire on the far end of the camp. It looked like my luck was holding. The few people that were out were concentrated down by the fire, leaving me more than half the camp to explore. I spotted a large silver airstream. It had a clown painted on the side, and I marked that as my first target. I was within twenty feet of it when a shadow detached from the side of a tent and intercepted me. It was a burly man with dark hair and sun-browned flesh. He had kind eyes but huge hands that looked gnarled from both hard work and bare-knuckle boxing. My martial arts training picked up the way he moved and the lightness of his step despite the weight of heavy muscle on his frame. He was at least two decades older and forty pounds heavier than me and he worried me more than Lazlo did. This man would be able to fight, and fight well.

I plastered a smile on my face, "Hey! Just taking the walk from my trailer and couldn't help but notice the lovely art on some of these trailers," I absently turned to gesture at a wagon to my left, it had a crude painting of a man covered in jigsaw tattoos and entwined with snakes. I noticed several shadowy shapes walking toward us from the fire and knew I only had a minute or so to talk my way past this guy and disappear into the dusk. If I could get out clean, I could swing back later in the night.

"No bullshit from you. Cannot lie to a Rom boy," he shook his head; his expression said he was disappointed in me. His accent was nearly identical to Henry's, Bela Lugosi with some harder Zs and Vs.

"Alright, you got me," change of tact, time to pull out the stalker, no harm no foul, "I'm a huge fan of Skylar Monroe and I just wanted to meet her. But like, no harm no foul, right? I mean I didn't even see her and I'll gladly just go." He made a barking sound and I realized it was a laugh. The pause stopped me from bolting however.

"You think me very stupid no? Monroe's very famous; they're up front on the road so all can see who enter camp. You cannot miss them on way into camp. So this second lie, plus you not see so well but I see you very well back at the tent. I think you very foolish boy."

Saw me back at the tent? My mind raced, I had hardly noticed the workmen, only the giant Lazlo. Then I remembered the one man other than Henry to whom he'd been deferential. An older man who might be the man before me, but I had never seen his face. I swore under my breath and turned to run. Plan A was garbage.

Massive hands closed on my shoulders and as I was turned into the grinning face of Lazlo, the giant hammered one of his fists into my guts and I dropped like a stone. The air hissed out of my lungs and my entire dinner slewed around in my guts. I had to fight not to throw it all up.

"Lazlo, no! Not in the camp. This man has made a mistake and simply needs to be escorted out."

The huge hands grabbed me again and pulled me back to my feet. I was turned to face the first man. The other shadows had arrived, another four men, each looking more dangerous than the last. To put it mildly, things were not going well for me. One of the men was fondling a knife and I couldn't help but notice that all of them had blades on their hips. Not small folders, either. These were big knives any Marine would be proud to carry into the field.

Lazlo heaved me off the ground and I don't know why, but Plan B flashed through my mind. I started shouting.

"You can't take me. I want the clown, give me the clown. I want the bastard who steals kids. You give the bastard to me or I'll go through you all. The clown!" Lazlo's hand clamped over my mouth and I bit my tongue, blood flooded my mouth and I knew what I needed to do.

"What do you want me to do to him now, Ben?" Lazlo's voice rumbled right through my body. He really did have something in his chest. It was bizarre, but I was more worried about what was about to happen. I needed to play this right.

"Stupid boy, you threaten one Rom you threaten all the Romany," Ben flicked his glance back toward the Airstream with the clown painted on it. I could see lights on in several of the surrounding wagons, including it. Faces in the windows like black smudges. "I think Lazlo that you shall remove this boy from our camp, perhaps as far as the woods and there you will teach him a lesson in threatening. A lesson can only be learned by the living, Gabriel." Ben turned hard eyes on the man holding the knife. "There will be no death tonight."

Gabriel, I guess that was his name, nodded and sheathed the blade.

"You are a foolish boy," Ben said, turning back to me, "but never say that the Rom don't teach."

I bit Lazlo's hand and the giant slipped his grip. I have no idea where his hands had been but they tasted awful and his flesh was cold. I fought my gag reflex; this was my last chance. I shouted, "He's a monster, a monster." I managed to get a few more words out before the big man punched me in the gut a second time and then I lost the battle I'd won earlier. My dinner ended up all over Lazlo's boots as I collapsed into a shuddering heap.

Ben grunted in disgust and swore in his native tongue. "Take him out of my camp. We can all be monsters, boy. Make it a tough lesson but a fair one."

Lazlo grabbed the back of my head and the other four each grabbed a limb and they pretty much just ran me back up the hill, out of the camp, up the grass, and into the deeper shadows of the tree line.

To the untrained eye I then preceded to get my ass beat. While I would never call myself a master, I have achieved the rank of master in aikido. I rolled with the punches and I redirected my attacker's energies around me. Several times they struck each other harder than they hit me. I even took a few chances to use skeletal-joint locks on the gypsies to drag them around and dump them again and again. I managed to avoid the huge form of Lazlo, turning most of his blows towards the others. But in order for this to work, I couldn't be the victor.

I sold it with everything I had. Every glancing blow that struck home, I screamed or cringed or threw myself on the ground. The bite to my tongue was bleeding freely and I spat as much blood around as possible. The messier the better. It was a hell of a show but I'd have rather been watching it instead of taking the beating.

Several of their strikes landed with more than enough force to do damage. I took an elbow that broke my nose, mashed flat and bleeding, and I was in trouble. My breathing was disrupted. I dropped into a heap and they boot-stomped me for a few moments and then stopped. Their breathing was ragged and one of them knelt down and checked my pulse. He grunted, apparently satisfied that I would live based off the twenty seconds worth of finger pressure on my neck.

Someone spat on me and the rest laughed and walked away. I waited a full minute before I rolled over and stood up. My face hurt like hell and I was certain that my good looks were ruined by the broken nose. I moved off the trail and waited. I had a hunch and I really hoped I was right; otherwise, I had taken a beating for nothing.

It was a full ten minutes later before I heard the first footsteps in the brush and I tensed. I had guessed correctly. I'd hoped that the killer—and I was convinced that the clown was a killer—had heard me shouting. It was a foolish plan, but I figured that anyone who preyed on kids wouldn't have a problem with trying his hand at attacking a beaten and battered man. I was not ready for what stepped into the clearing. It really was a clown.

In full makeup.

10

Seriously. A clown. He was in his full get-up, baggy silk clothes in a gaudy mish mash of colors, huge shoes, and full on grease-paint. The white of his face was luminous in the dark stand of trees. It was just past sundown and in the shadows it was as dark as full night.

The pattern of the clown's face was made up of geometrical shapes. He had a red circle on his forehead, a blue and yellow diamond one-color around each eye, and a green square over his lips. It was a truly bizarre sight, and I have to admit, I froze.

The clown paused and crouched, he ran his gloved hand through the trampled grass of the clearing. I started to wonder if I'd attracted a clown, or some kind of Native American tracker. I reached down to my right shin. I had an extendable baton strapped there. Spring-loaded solid steel and it packed a hell of a kick.

Something dark was smeared on the clown's white gloves. The clown sniffed his fingers and then sucked them clean. I was glad I had already puked up my dinner as I felt my stomach roil. The bastard was licking my blood. He snuffled the air like a dog and then fell to his knees and buried his face in the grass.

Flecks of my blood decorated his white mask as he raised his head. He stared directly into my patch of shadows. This guy was a total freak and I'd waited long enough. I smashed the bottom of the baton into the ground and the eight-inch tube extended to eighteen. I leapt out of the brush and might have recoiled in mid-air, if that were physically possible. For a single second, the eyes that looked up at me had seemed feral, their cores glowing red.

Since I didn't have *ACME air brakes*, I finished my jump and crashed the steel baton down toward the back of the clown's skull.

The back of the head is a damn hard target, but the wrong strike can kill. I wasn't thinking about it and I didn't pull the blow.

WHAM! It was as if I had slammed into a wall. The shock of the blow traveled up my arm and the pain of it lanced through my palm. The clown grunted at the impact and then stood as I backed away. That was not possible. It came at me with arms upraised, hands grasping, and I stepped into its charge, not away.

I cracked the baton into the inside of the man's left arm, moving that limb out of the way while I turned my shoulder into his chest. I dropped the baton and grabbed the right arm at the wrist and elbow, pivoting my body—clown's arm over my shoulder, my back into his chest—I dropped down and threw Bozo over my body. Textbook, quick and clean.

The muscles in his arm were like cabled steel under my hands and the bulk of the man was surprising. He wasn't fat but he was damn dense, heavily muscled and I had to adjust accordingly. For a moment I wondered if I had a PCP freak on my hands. I twisted the wrist into a painful lock that should have put Mr. Universe down, or at least kept him under control.

Not so Mr. Clown. He twisted his wrist in a savage tug that broke my lock and for the second time, my mind registered that the move should have been impossible. He then shoved me away, his palm striking my chest so hard I thought I'd been hit with a bat. After the previous beating, my body was not happy with me and I dropped on suddenly weak legs.

I rolled across the clearing and forced myself back to my feet as the clown also stood. We faced each other across the clearing and I wished that I had kept my hands on the baton. Then again, this fight shouldn't be happening. The guy must have had a steel plate in the back of his skull.

A smile stretched across his face and I realized that he wasn't even breathing hard. He wasn't in any way affected by the blow to his head, the throw, or even the pain of my joint lock. Christ, at the least I expected the man to be massaging his damn arm.

"You have no idea what you're messing with," his voice was deeper than I'd expected. Then again clowns never speak, so what exactly was I expecting the voice to *be* like? The man was a gym rat at the very least, if not an actual bodybuilder. He might not sound like a clown, but his voice meshed perfectly with my image of a steroid using muscle-bound ape.

He came at me in a flurry of swipes. He didn't throw punches, he just slapped with his huge arms. I hadn't taken many hits to the head yet, but I would swear that my eyes were playing tricks on me. As I blocked and weaved and tossed him aside it seemed to me that his mouth was far wider than a normal person's should be. Also that red glow was back into his eyes, and this time there wasn't the reflection of the moon to account for it. His arms seemed to move within ghostly images; like old, bad kung fu movies where they slowed the film just enough that you would see like twenty images of the guy's arms swinging through the air.

I shook my head and the wavering arms solidified. I was definitely going to need to see a doctor after this job was over. He rushed me and I swung him around, sending him head first into a tree. He finally staggered, taking a step away from the tree and then leaned against it. I grinned. There were dark streaks in his makeup and I wondered if I had finally made the bastard bleed.

"What did you do with the boys? Where are Jacob and Tommy?"

The clown laughed; at least I assumed it was a laugh. It was guttural and harsh. He said a single word, "Bittersweet."

"What? Just tell me what you did with them and then we can end this." I needed to end this. I couldn't dance around with the brute all night.

"The older boy was bitter, so full of rage and anger and sorrow. While the little boy… he was sooooo sweet." The raw lust in that voice instantly had me shaking in rage. I reached for my gun and suddenly the clown wasn't standing by the tree anymore.

He was right on top of me.

He wrenched my right arm out of my jacket, the socket popping with a loud crack as he dislocated my shoulder, almost breaking my collarbone with the savagery of the attack. His right hand closed on my throat and he slammed me into a tree. The wind was knocked out of my lungs and he squeezed my throat tight before I could draw a breath. Spots swam before my eyes and he brought his face close to mine.

"I ate them." He whispered it into my ear, blowing hot breath along my neck. The words shocked through my skull and images burst before my eyes, images I couldn't control of the meat being dressed and prepped for feast. Of the clown taking a bite out of the still-screaming boy to taste the fear, taste the raw flesh. "They were so very good and I'm so very full, otherwise I would have slaughtered you already. But there is no need."

The voice was clotted with evil, dark lust, and insanity. The clown leaned forward and licked my face. I shrieked and the bastard sank teeth into my cheek. The pain was searing, I felt every nerve in my body ignite as he bit into my flesh. He only marked me, but I knew I was very close to having my entire cheek torn from my face. I felt hot blood running down my chin as he drew away from me, then I lashed out with head. My temple smashed into his nose and I saw black for a second. Christ, the man's head was as hard as stone and I was almost positive I'd only given myself a concussion.

He laughed again and eased up his grip on my neck. I lashed out with my left hand, raking my fingers over his face, driving for his eyes. He hissed in surprise and let me go, actually jumping away from me. I'd finally hurt him.

He roared and shook his head. I hoped that the bastard was blinded. He glared at me as I fumbled to draw my gun with my left hand, but it is nearly impossible to draw a gun out of your left armpit with your left arm. I caught sight of his face then, and I froze. The moon was bright, and we'd stepped from the shadows into a clearing, where he was caught perfectly in a silvery shaft of light. The greasepaint was wiped away in a large swath from forehead down to upper lip, one eye squinted shut. The flesh revealed underneath, while still having paint in the creases and thinly coated overall, was a deep shade of purple. Not the deep black purple of eggplant but purple like a royal robe. I wanted it to be another layer of paint but it made no sense for my clawing hands to have only removed one layer if there were more beneath. It also didn't make sense to put down a very dark layer of paint to only put white on top of it.

"What the fuck are you?" was all I managed to get out before he was back on me. I took a punch to the ribs that broke them easily, the fierce burn in my chest and the sudden taste and smell of blood had me convinced that my lung was pierced. I was deeply screwed and I needed an exit. I kneed the clown in the nuts.

Again I felt like I was kicking a tree or stone, but this time I had the satisfaction of seeing him stagger back. As hard as his skin seemed to be, he was soft in the eyes and the balls.

As fast as possible I used my left hand to lift my right to the butt of the Kimber and I drew the gun. I then transferred the gun from my right hand to my left and pointed it at the clown. I had trained to shoot left-handed, just in case, but I was still horrible at it. It made me pause as I considered what was about to happen. I was running on pure adrenaline and the first stages of shock. My body was no longer telling me where it hurt.

I had never fired a gun at a person in my life and had never really expected to do so. Yeah, I had always wanted to be a soldier, be a warrior, but I had reconciled myself to a reality where it wasn't likely. His cries had been loud enough that the camp had to have been alerted; if not the circus, then the other people should have heard something.

I hesitated for a second longer and then the image of Tommy smiling his gap-toothed smile and trying to set me up with his mother came to mind. The bastard had confessed to eating a six-year-old child and although I might not be able to prove it, I could do something about it. I pulled the trigger.

I was unsteady in both my aim and my footing. I was hurt but I yanked on the trigger until the slide locked back and the last shell was spinning through the air. He was only a few yards in front of me and I had trained for hundred-foot pistol shots. Ten of my fifteen rounds hit the clown. Most of them went into the center of the chest, a few into the arms, and one into the left thigh.

I walked forward, smoothly pulling the trigger, he staggered back as each bullet tore into him. He dropped to the ground and I thrust the gun at his face. It was empty and with my useless right arm there was no way for me to reload a magazine. There was a lack of blood which surprised me. Then again, I was conditioned to accept movie gunshots as the real thing.

The clown snarled and slapped the gun out of my hand. I watched it sail into the air and disappear into the brush. A part of me wailed, as I had several grand invested in the gun, the other part of me was aware that the clown was trying to get up again. This situation was completely wrong, the laws of the world no longer made sense.

There were no purple-skinned people eaters who were strong as hell and bulletproof. It just didn't happen in a sane world. The shout of voices in the distance swung both of our gazes away. The clown seemed to fear discovery as much as I did. I could only hope that he was mortally wounded and just too stupid to realize it. Even if he wasn't, I was hurt bad and probably not going to make it unless I got the hell out of there. I still didn't understand the circus, but I understood that they looked after their own and the clown was one of their own. I wondered if they knew what he had done. If so, I would have to deal with an entire troupe.

The fact that the clown was crawling away from the voices made me believe otherwise. He was hiding among them. I staggered into the trees, hoping that my addled brain could remember the way back to my car.

I bounced off trees and tried desperately to cling to my path. Away from the circus camp, it had to be away. I was certain that if they found me, I would never be seen again. Even if it was just to hide the evidence. The Romany, the Gypsy, had a bad rap throughout Europe; I was certain they would do anything to save face here in America.

I stumbled out of the trees and rolled down a sharp incline. I tripped again as I climbed to my feet and I could only use my left arm to arrest my fall. I climbed up a bank and hit a wooden post. It was rough as I ran my hand to the top and felt a cross beam—the wooden barrier that ran along the parking area.

I was sobbing in relief as I pulled myself over the rail and fell into a heap on the gravel road. I was blinded by lights and then thankful for the slight squeal of brakes. A car door opened.

"Holy…! Hey mister, are you ok?" I raised a hand toward the voice, toward the light. I was seeing double as a black shape materialized into a man in a red-checkered shirt who dropped to his knees in the sharp gravel to check my pulse. The look on his face wasn't comforting, but the cell phone he placed to his ear was. "Yeah, my name is Kevin Moss and I need an ambulance…."

They were the sweetest words I'd ever heard and with them said I allowed myself to drift into unconsciousness.

11

That was my first time in the hospital—July of last year. I want to preface this with a single note—I was medicated and possibly concussed, so please don't judge too harshly. I did and thought a lot of stupid things as I woke in the hospital.

It was a nice place called St. Francis. I remember I came to in a bed. My right arm was back in the socket and strapped firmly to my chest. Bandages covered the side of my face and two fingers on my left hand were splinted. I had no recollection of breaking my fingers.

I was only hooked up to an IV. At least I wasn't handcuffed to the bed; I rolled to my side and reached for the nightstand. The motion caused my head to swim and I fought back a lump in my throat that I knew would turn into dry heaves if I allowed it. I pulled open the drawer on the nightstand and was relieved to find my wallet and car keys, also my empty holster. I mourned the loss of my gun, but right now I had to worry about how to explain my presence in the woods.

I was certain that as soon as the nurses discovered I was awake, there would be a bunch of cops in my room asking me all sorts of questions. I was just thinking of what to say when the curtain around my bed was whisked away and a pretty woman stepped in.

"Well, Mr. Shaw, we're finally awake? Very good. How do you feel today?" She asked the questions in a friendly manner, but still went about her job efficiently, ruthlessly. She pushed my drawer closed with her hip, pushed me onto my back and put one of those thermometer strips across my forehead. She took my pulse, a pleasant smile plastered on her face as she looked at her watch.

"Ummm, tired and my head is fuzzy. Where the heck am I?" I

was going to play up the head wound as much as possible.

“You have a mild concussion, so your head should be muddy for a bit, but you’ll be fine. You’re at St. Francis in Poughkeepsie. You remember what you were doing the other night? Pulse and temp are good.” She checked the IV, made an adjustment to the tubing.

“I don’t know what day it is today.” It was true, her use of “other night” made me think it might be Monday. “I don’t remember much of anything other than going out to camp for my vacation.” I had a really bad idea and I hoped it would work.

“Vacation?” Her eyes flickered over to the drawer and then back to me. “Well, you seem to be in better health now. There are some gentlemen who want to see you. I guess I’ll be sending them in.”

The last wasn’t a question and she whisked out of the room as I wondered how long I’d have before a cop was standing at my bed. It wasn’t nearly as long as I’d hoped. My idea to change the chart—again I stress head trauma and pain meds don’t mix well—on my bed wasn’t going to happen. Did the cops already know my name? That seemed a stupid question, but since I still had my wallet and such I figured that they might have respected my privacy, or at the least hadn’t run it yet. I snorted a laugh and regretted it almost immediately; something in my broken nose throbbed in pain and tears welled in my eyes. Of course they had run my ID, the hospital wanted to get paid and I hadn’t been awake to fill out an admittance form. Also, as the victim of a violent crime the police would have to make reports, and with an empty holster, it was guaranteed that they ran my out-of-state license and matched it to my gun registration. All of that went through my head and I still proceeded like a total idiot.

I surveyed the room. There was a second bed—thankfully empty—and two of everything: two TVs, two guest chairs, two bedside tables, and a row of dressers split in the center. If I’d been back home, the hospital there would have put your clothes—assuming they didn’t have to cut them from you or burn them—in a bag at the bottom of one of the drawers. I wondered if it was the same at St. Francis. I was weighing how much trouble I would get into if I just grabbed my clothes and ran.

I wondered what the final charges would look like. At the very least I was getting the idea that my first case might be my last. Right now *I* was the victim of a crime, but at that moment my brain was only thinking of guilt and flight. It was in full-on panic mode. I would find out later that it was an interaction between the drugs in my system that made me paranoid.

I was about to make my move, my hand poised to yank the IV out of my hand, when the door to my room slid open. I froze and the gentleman in the door gave me half a smile, one that pulled at one corner of his mouth and never touched his eyes, a perfunctory, pre-programmed motion. I eased back into my bed with a barely-breathed sigh. My panic swelled.

I knew he was a cop. He was plainclothes so I put him right at detective. The gears in my head started spinning and I had a load of bullshit ready. He looked like a hard man. His black suit was rumpled and well worn and he didn't wear a tie. The top button of his shirt was open. He had cold, grey eyes that said he'd seen fifty or more years of bullshit, but thick black hair that looked naturally dark, not a grey hair in sight. His cheeks had scars across them, single knife slashes running from his ears to his chin. A scar knotted the hollow of his throat and I almost let the bullshit go; I almost just gave in. This was a hard man. Then I thought about a purple-skinned man—monster—that claimed to have eaten two children. I didn't have time to be locked in a cell, or words to explain the situation that wouldn't mark me as a nut case.

The cop tried a smile again. He pulled a notebook out of his pocket and flipped it open. I was pleased to see it was the same kind I carried.

"Mr. Shaw," he looked at the paper and then back at me. "So, no bullshit, you want to explain who you are and why someone, or ones, kicked your ass?"

"Well it's all really fuzzy, Officer…?" I was going to have to fall back on the concussion to help flesh this out. My mind was racing to come up with a good answer, and despite the fact that I was certain he knew exactly who—or at the least what—I was, I still had a solid line of bullshit coming to the ready.

"Detective, Ian Buntline. I know you've suffered some head trauma, Mr. Shaw, but let's all cut the crap. I have more important cases to work. So I want the bullet points. Who you are? Why were you at the campground and why were you wearing an empty holster? I have men running through those woods looking for a crime scene. Why don't you give me some peace of mind?" He wrote something in his notebook.

I took a deep breath and tried to keep a straight face. "Look, I seriously don't have a clue as to all the details. I'm on vacation, looking to camp out. I must have walked into something when I was hiking through the woods. I don't remember. I'm a co...," I just stopped myself from making a mistake, I was seconds away from claiming to be a cop, to rattling off Olaf's badge number. That might have worked better if they hadn't already known my name and known exactly who I was. My frickin PI's license is actually in front of my Driver's. Next time I hunt down a killer, I'll leave my ID behind in my car. All these great tips, after the fact. I coughed to cover my mistake and continued. "I'm just a man on vacation, fully licensed to carry a firearm, who must have walked in on something. Whoever attacked me has my gun."

"Just a *normal* guy, in the woods, with a *gun*?" His tone said he didn't believe me at all, but I knew it was a fear of a lot of cops, their service piece falling into the hands of a criminal and being used for God knew what. He looked me over; I could only imagine what he saw. Most of me was strapped and wrapped in bandages, I only had one usable arm and it was my off side. I tried to look as pathetic as possible. "So you always bring your sidearm with you on vacation? In a shoulder rig with three loaded clips?" He flipped open his notebook and read something, "Also something strapped to his ankle, a knife or can of mace? Three different knives and a multi-tool? Seems a lot for a hike, and not even a single bottle of water or a map or a compass?"

"Yeah, I was a boy scout. Always be prepared. Knife is the best thing you can have when in the woods and a multi-tool is even better. If it was hunting season, I'd have had a rifle too." I tried to smile but it actually hurt my face and pulled at the tape covering the bitten cheek.

He nodded slowly and then began to write a series of lines in his notebook. He looked me over and then without another word, he turned on his heel and left the room. I didn't have a clue as to why he left the room. I was just glad he had. The paranoia fully spiked and I went into panic mode. I had managed to stop myself from several bad lies, but I didn't think I would be able to hold off for much longer. This next part is a little embarrassing.

I had to yank the IV out of my arm with my teeth and I was out of the bed in an instant. I glanced around the curtain and out my door. It was clear. A few nurses down the hall were having a conversation, but no cop stood guard, and Buntline wasn't in the hall. My head swam, spots revolving before my eyes, and I almost fell back into the bed. I had gotten up far too fast, but I had to move.

I pulled open the top drawer of the dresser which was filled with gauze and tape and tools. The second drawer was empty, but the third one had my boots and pants. Apparently my shirt had been cut or thrown away. Next to the pants was a white robe. From a distance it might fool someone into thinking it was a lab coat.

The pants were baggy cargo type and I could slip them on without unbuttoning them. The belt was the only thing that held them on. I liked them because they allowed me to strike and move with ease. I stepped into the pants and pulled them up with the belt. It was a little strange trying to tighten the belt in the wrong direction with my left hand.

This was going to be the worst escape in history. I tucked my feet into my boots, thankful they were the type with the zipper hidden on the side so I didn't need to unlace or tie them. It was once again awkward as hell trying to reach around my legs with my left hand and pull the zipper on the right side of my right leg, but I managed.

With the robe around my shoulders, I stepped out of my room and turned away from the nurse's station, heading deeper into the wing. I saw a sign for stairs and I hobbled along toward it. The initial rush of adrenaline had propelled me out of bed, but was now abandoning me to the aches and the pain. I felt like I'd been through ten tournaments of kendo without wearing my padding. I think even my hair hurt.

The door was getting closer and I focused all of my energy on it. Another door to my right opened and a cop stepped out. She was in uniform and she filled it rather well, blonde hair piled in a braid at the back of her head and very blue eyes, the first thing I noticed. Her hands were full of coffee cups. *Just cause she's a cop doesn't mean she has any clue who you are* flitted through my head. I took another step.

"I'd hate to drop all these coffees and have to tase you, Mr. Shaw."

Shit.

I spun and started back toward my room. She stepped up behind me. "I hope you like your coffee with cream and sugar," she said drily behind me.

Buntline was leaning against my door. He had a look on his face that was part amused and part disgusted. "Nice hustle, Jon. I wish you hadn't just proved me right. I think we have a long discussion ahead of us."

We were apparently on a first-name basis now. I hobbled past him into the room, pausing to kick off my boots and drop the robe. I slid into bed in my pants.

"First, I want to thank you," Buntline said, "for not giving Officer Rook an issue. I'd be a lot angrier with you if she had dropped my coffee." He paused to accept a cup from the pretty, young officer. She put a cup on the dinner tray on the rolling cart next to my bed, then pushed the cart toward me. She had solid, farm-girl good looks and I wished I'd met her under different circumstances. "Also lucky for you, I'm willing to cut you some slack due to the concussion. Until this little stunt you were the victim of a crime, now I need convincing that is true."

I sipped my coffee first, trying to think it through. He was a hard man and I had no doubt that even in my current state he would have taken a shot at me. I looked him over again, trying to get a feel for him. He was a *solid* man, the best words I could think of were *solid* and *square*. He had a square chin and broad shoulders, a deep chest and a waist that didn't taper but was squared away like the rest of him. It could have been from wearing a bulletproof vest but I was pretty sure it was all him.

"I panicked. Sorry, I don't know what's going through my mind. I'm sorry about how I'm handling this. I'm a private investigator looking into a missing kid case. The local PD was dragging their asses and another kid went missing. I traced it to a man in the circus and decided to come out here and rattle some cages. I rattled and took a beating from a bunch of gypsies, nothing major other than the nose." I took another sip of the coffee. As Officer Rook went to the door and took up her post as guardian, I watched her go.

"Continue," he said, dragging my attention back from Officer Rook.

"Well, I took the beating because I thought it would draw out the man I was looking for." That brought Rook back into the room and she leaned against the door. She seemed intrigued by someone who would take a beating deliberately. Buntline did too, but I could tell by his gaze that baiting criminals was old hat to him. "The bastard came and he took me apart. I have no idea what he's on, but it must be steroids and painkillers. Things went a little crazy, my head really is muddy, but the bastard admitted to killing the kids and things just… blur." No way was I mentioning purple skin or glowing red eyes.

"So you're fighting this guy and he just admits that he killed a bunch of kids?" Buntline made notes.

"No, *Ian*. I mean the bastard pulls my arm out of its socket and he picks me up with one hand around my throat. While he's choking me, the bastard tells me, right into my ear… he tells me that he ATE the KIDS." My voice rose sharply and Officer Rook slid the door closed with a solid thump. She looked nervous. But Buntline seemed unmoved.

"So now we have a cannibal carnie?" he asked drily.

I glared at him. Why had I trusted this cop? I knew no one would believe me. My anger got the better of me, "Yeah, a cannibal.

That's what he told me, right before he took a bite out of me." I tore the bandage off my face, ignoring the sting as tape yanked at hair and flesh. I had no idea what I looked like, but I remembered the pain as the clown sank his teeth into me. He'd gone deep, but just held his jaws there, marking me, but not tearing the muscle away from my face. Rook had had enough; she left the room again, closing the door behind her.

The look on Buntline's face softened. His own experiences and pain playing in the depths of his grey eyes. We shared a moment. The anger drained out of my body and my muscles relaxed. I had pushed the painkillers to their limits and now my aches and pains were setting off alarms throughout my body. Buntline opened his mouth but didn't say anything. He looked at his pad, perhaps seeking a question or a clue. The door opened with authority and a slim, dark-skinned man in a white lab coat came into the room.

He moved at a rapid pace, efficient, no motion wasted. He had a look of stern disapproval on his face and his glare was first directed at Buntline, but he still had a bit of anger left for me. "I think all parties need to lower the stress levels. This is a hospital not an interrogation room. You need rest, Mr. Shaw."

I was impressed that he knew my name without looking at my chart. He whisked the chart off the end of my bed and walked to my side. He shook his head as he looked at me and I actually felt a blush of guilt. He grabbed my wrist in a firm grip and took my pulse. "I am Doctor Nehru. You have sustained many injuries, which I am sure is why the police are here, but you need some rest. So please be keeping the questioning to a manageable level and a volume that is more courteous to the others on the ward. I am clear?" He glared at both of us again and released my wrist. "Now officer, if you will permit me a few moments with my patient. Also, you should check your blood pressure; your color is most displeasing."

Buntline backed off a few steps and sat on the edge of the dresser. He sipped his coffee without comment and then he flipped open his phone. He turned away from us and began to talk in a hushed voice.

"Well, I guess that is as good as we'll be allowed. Now Mr. Shaw, it is a pleasure to be seeing you up and about, but in your condition I must ask that you remain in bed and only walk the halls after receiving permission to do so. You have many injuries and I'm sure you are concerned for them. You suffered a minor concussion and it looks very good that you will recover fully from it. However, if you have trouble with bright lights, dizziness, or spatial awareness, you must be seeing your physician immediately."

His voice was a blend of cultured English, like Oxford English, and Indian and it sort of *burred* out of him. It made me think of the giant Lazlo, though opposite here as it was comforting and amusing trying to follow his words, whereas with the giant roustabout it had been an artificial droning that was eerie at best.

He smiled at me and gesturing toward my wrapped arm. "Now the good news. There is no break in your clavicle, just a very minor crack. The dislocation is worse, but your X-rays show previous scar tissue, so I assume that you've suffered this injury before?"

I nodded, "Yeah, I've had my arm dislocated a time or two. Overzealous student, badly preformed *shihonage* and *POP* goes the shoulder."

He nodded, but said nothing for a moment. We heard a loud snort from Buntline, but he was still on the phone and his comment wasn't for us. The Doctor frowned at the cop and then turned back to me.

"An actual break would have had your arm immobilized for a month and therapy for weeks afterward, plus constant X-rays to make sure the bone reconnected properly. As is, I believe you'll only need two weeks in the sling and then another two of taking it easy and performing some light exercises. So none of this *show-nagee*, whatever.... You will need new X-rays at the end of the two weeks to make sure that you are ready for the rehab; otherwise you'll just make it all worse. Your face seems to be healing fine, no sign of infection. Either way, I'll be prescribing some anti-inflammatory and some antibiotics just in case. You'll have some scarring, but we managed to straighten out your nose." With nothing further to say, he made some scratches in the chart and then paused.

I realized he was giving me the chance to ask questions. Just as he started to move the synapses in my brain started firing again, "When can I get out of here then?"

"I would like to keep you for one more night. You've been unconscious for a full day and with the head trauma, I'm still a little concerned. The fact that your eyes are clearer and you're responsive is a very good sign. I'm predicting tomorrow morning." He hung the sign at the base of my bed and pocketed his pen.

"You said I was unconscious for a day. What day is today?"

"It's Tuesday, one o'clock to be precise," he glanced at his gold watch, smiled again, and then left the room, hurrying off for the next patient at the same rapid pace he'd entered.

Buntline was leaning against the dresser. His attention was back on me, and his expression was a neutral mask.

"So will I be able to leave tomorrow?" I wondered if I'd be handcuffed to the bed when he left.

"While you were talking with the doctor, I was making some calls. It seems that your story might have some bearing. A certain," he flipped open his notebook and checked over his scrawl, "Henry Holmes Circus was scheduled to grace our environs with its presence. They've left the city. All trace of them, other than some trash and refuse at a certain campground, has vanished. No explanation and some of their flyers are still up, but the circus is gone. Looks like they pulled out on Sunday night. Most of the campers didn't really notice the troupe leaving. They were more concerned with the gunshots from the woods."

The detective smiled at me, it was a mix between friendly and scary. I believe I got through to him then, the fact that I had been candid—I guess honesty really is the best policy. That someone else, an entire organization, looked to be the guilty party was in my favor. He was getting friendly, but still there was a feral hunter in him that was glaring out, that was open on his face as he spoke of the strange disappearance of hundreds of people, caravans, and semi-trucks.

"If they're running, then I doubt we'll find them in the state. As of right now I'm backing your story, but I'll tell you now that if I even find one hint of bullshit, I will be coming for you. You will find me on your doorstep."

He was a menacing prick but a good cop. I was already thinking about how I would find the circus again, when common sense kicked me. I had gone off to deal with the situation and nearly died. I was an amateur playing at detective but this was the real deal ahead of me. I needed to play straight or I would never survive the game.

"Hey, if it helps, I tracked them down by going to a website. Skylar Monroe is a model and contortionist that is working the circus, she keeps a blog and it mentions the itinerary. It got me here; maybe it'll have some half-assed excuse why they left and where they'll be." I tried to give him a winning smile, but with my battered face and the beginning of a wicked headache, I don't think it worked.

He nodded and wrote the information on his pad. He looked back up at me, the friendliness back in his eyes. "You're a pig-headed kid; I can see the stubbornness in your eyes. I'll let you know if I find them. Now then, how about descriptions of the men who attacked you and the clown…?"

So I eased back. A nurse came in and replaced the bandages on my face. She gave me a handful of Ibuprofen to knock out the swelling and dull the pain. I ran through the faces of the men as best I could remember, matching the names I'd heard as they talked in the parking lot and as they talked before and during my beating. Lazlo, the giant; Ben, the leader who hadn't participated; Gabriel, the man who played with his knife; Gunnar, Grigor, and Alexia, the thugs whose faces I couldn't pin to a name. I described Henry Holmes himself as well, stating that something about him didn't strike me as the violent type. Not that I wanted to protect a stranger but I didn't want the entire circus dragged down for thugs who thought they were doing good for the troupe.

The clown was the only one that truly had my ire. He was the one that needed to pay. Officer Rook rejoined us. She brought food for herself and Buntline. I had to make do with a tray from the cafeteria, though I'll admit that the food wasn't nearly as bad as I'd expected. Just watching them wolf down large burgers and what looked like hand-cut fries that made my inner fat child want to cry. Yummy Jell-O, sigh.

When I came to my final description, the clown himself, Buntline finally broke his relative silence. He hadn't commented during my entire description of the circus folk, merely ate his lunch with gusto. He was man who took large bites and relished each of them.

"Wait... he was a clown?" A fry stopped halfway to his mouth.

"How many times have I said he was a clown? It was a damn clown."

"I got that but I just never actually pictured... you know... Bozo kicking your ass." He grinned and tried to repress a laugh. "Sorry, I'm not laughing at you I'm just laughing at the image it's conjuring. You know, I just didn't think full makeup and a crazy wig."

I shook my head, "No wig, he was bald, covered in white greasepaint and had different colored geometric shapes on his face. He was in a baggy suit and I didn't notice if he wore damn clown shoes. Underneath the suit he was bodybuilder-jacked, all hard muscle and no fat. I'd put him at six foot four and about two-forty. Like I also said, I thought he was on drugs or something. I did some joint locks that should have had him staggering in pain and all he did was nearly break his own wrists still coming at me. This guy is a monster." I wanted to add one word "literally" but I was afraid of ruining what little rapport we'd built.

He choked back his humor, finished his lunch and wrote every detail he could squeeze out of me. Finally he'd gotten enough, stood up and pocketed the notebook. He stepped to the bed and I was surprised when he held out his hand. We shook.

"I'll be on top of this and I *will* let you know how it comes out." It was a vow; I had done something to earn this man's respect. As I looked closer at his face, I realized he wasn't entirely seeing me. Perhaps he was making the vow to me *and* to someone else, someone I reminded him of, a resurrected memory.

While I still had his hand, "Hey, you think you could get me a ride to my car tomorrow?" I tried another smile on him, my face twisting against bandages and swollen tissues.

He chuckled, "I'll have someone here to pick you up."

They left the room and despite an already-lost-day unconsciousness, I felt tired. I fought against the pull of sleep. Who knew I was in the hospital? My first answer was no one … I swore. Unless the cops called anyone to check up on me, such as my local PD or my father. Pushing thirty and still I was concerned with making him proud and worried about pissing him off. If my mother found out I was in the hospital, she'd go crazy with worry which would upset my old man and he'd beat my ass once I was healed enough. I chuckled.

I relaxed, letting everything go. Time to rest. I knew that Buntline would fail. Knew the circus had left the state, left his sphere of influence. Anything else would be too easy. The best I could hope for would be to find out about their next stop. Not that it mattered, as it would be at least a month before I could do anything, and I *was* going to do something. I was not done.

I whispered my vow into the room, "I will hunt you down. I will make you confess, and I will bury you. I swear on the lives of Jacob Carpenter and Tommy Mathers that I will not rest until I've ended your sickness. I am Jon Shaw, I am a monster hunter."

I slept, thankfully free of dreams.

12

I don't know why every hospital insists that you leave in a wheel-chair. Who came up with that rule? They were nice enough to give me a free T-shirt, at least I thought it was free. Knowing my luck it was probably going to show up on my hospital bill and cost me forty dollars. I was slightly grouchy as an orderly pushed me to the front doors. I felt better, but I was unhappy that I couldn't use my right arm at all.

Luckily they had unstrapped me and allowed me to wear a sling. The pain had been so intense that a nurse had had to help me into the T-shirt. I was already thinking about how much it would hurt trying to remove that shirt when I was home alone. I guess the gift shop didn't have any button-downs.

I lost my grouchy attitude when the sun hit me and I saw Officer Rook leaning against the hood of her black and white. She cut a nice figure in her uniform, though I would have loved to see her hair down. I couldn't stop the smile that flashed across my face.

She pushed off the hood and turned to the passenger-side door. I don't know if it was purely a product of my ego, but I thought I saw a blush and smile on her face as she turned her back to me. I hit the brakes on the wheelchair and pushed myself up with my one arm. Hurt like hell, but I wouldn't let either of them know it.

I eased past her and into the car and she hurried around to the driver's side. I wondered if she'd volunteered or was simply obeying Buntline. As she closed the door I said, "Thank you, Officer Rook."

"Call me Ana." She fired the ignition, dropped the car into drive and pulled off the curb, all in a single motion that put me into the seat, squealed the tires, and sent us hurtling toward traffic. Holy hell, the farm girl liked to speed. She rapidly flipped the siren on and off, traffic parted just in time for her to slip through. I was scared and turned on at the same time. She'd given me her first name. Interesting.

The car fishtailed as she slid into the lane and hurtled down the road. We were rushing past forty and we'd only just cleared the parking lot. She kept her eyes on the road but turned enough to flash me a grin. In the sunlight I noticed a dusting of freckles across her nose and cheeks.

Was this the secret of Private Investigators? As soon as you get your PI license you're immediately surrounded by beautiful women? My client, her neighbor, and now this cop. Hell, what would have happened if I had met the contortionist? For the first time in over a week I felt like laughing. I grinned, and allowed myself that small pleasure. It was nice to just let all the stress flow away, all the fear and anger, gone.

We made it to the campground in record time and I was kind of disappointed by that. I wanted to spend more time with this woman—Ana—but she seemed in a rush. Besides, I needed to get back home.

She slowed down on the dirt and gravel paths and pulled up right beside my car without me telling her which one was mine. Considering it was the only one in the area with Connecticut plates, it wasn't that hard to spot.

"Fun ride?" she smiled again, her eyes flicking over mine but not staying in contact.

"I wasn't expecting NASCAR, but yeah, that was some killer driving. Did anything pan out yet on the investigation?" I wanted to delay my departure but I also wanted more information.

"Looks like they left the state. Ian won't stop though, he has a lot of connections. He used to be a big-deal cop out of the City." I could hear the capital C in City, she was only talking about New York. "So he still has some pull. This is as close as Ian will probably ever get to retirement, working mid-state. He'll find the circus." She turned more toward me, slightly shy, not something you expect out of a cop.

I reached into my coat and pulled out a business card—nothing ventured, nothing gained, "Look, if anything comes up, or for *any other* reason, you can give me a call." I placed the card directly into her palm and made sure my hand lingered longer than it needed. She smiled and this time her gaze held my own.

"I have something for you," she said.

I was intrigued; she reached over the seat and pulled a bag from the backseat onto her lap. She unzipped the bag, saying, "Normally you wouldn't get this, but when Ian saw it he realized it would mean a lot to you." She pulled out a plastic baggie covered in writing. Inside was my Kimber.

I was surprised at the thrill that shot through me. I had spent a lot of money and a lot of time on that gun. She ripped the bag open and handed the gun to me, followed by the empty magazine. I slipped the gun into my coat pocket and opened the door to the car. If I stayed a moment longer, I might do something stupid like try to kiss her.

As I closed the door she rolled down the window and handed me *her* card. "Just in case you're back in my area." She winked and then threw the car into reverse. She pulled out and swung the car around in a blast of dirt and gravel, and I shied away. She was a wild one. Her personal number was scrawled across the back of the card.

Perks of the job, perks of the job.

I got my ass in my car and headed back to Connecticut.

13

Recovery. What a pain. I hate not being able to do anything, not that I was a hundred percent hampered, it was just that everything I wanted to do was affected by the shoulder.

I couldn't train, at least not fully. I did spend a good amount of time swinging the Jo staff and Bokken with my left arm only. Working only one side of my body, while good at shoring up that weakness, didn't benefit me overall. With only one hand, I couldn't even clean my pistol which sorely needed it. I had to face my father, who hadn't told my mother anything, as it turned out. When I arrived at the house she completely freaked out on me. It was bad.

After the mandatory emotional meltdown and screaming fit, she babied me. I was fed to near bursting and my father took care of the gun cleaning for me. After that I was ready for the harder challenge.

When I arrived on Erin Carpenter's porch. I had a fresh bandage on my face; I didn't want her seeing the puffy bruised flesh or the scabbed teeth marks. I only wish I had an eye patch. The concussion had bloomed one of my eyes full of blood, it was horrific.

It must have been even worse than I thought. When the door opened, she burst into tears. I held her with my one good arm and walked her into the house, closing the door behind me. How much worse would it be?

"I'm sorry." That was all I got to say before she sagged against me. I thought she might have fainted but she'd just gone slack. Drained. Only hope had held her up and I had just cut it away from her. I brought her into the living room, not an easy task with the one arm and all the other aches and pains. Somehow I managed to get her onto the couch, wrapped in a blanket and huddled against my side.

I didn't want to tell her the rest and in the end I decided to change the truth. I didn't tell her that Tommy was gone too; I didn't mention him at all. I told her about the fight with the clown and the fleeing circus. I played up the hunter's instinct I sensed in Ian and how he'd scour the state. I told her that I wasn't done yet and that I would bring pain back onto the man who had hurt her.

Erin wasn't the "eye for an eye" type and I don't think my words truly gave her comfort, but my presence was a balm. I stayed with her and gave her what comfort I could.

14

Two weeks was hell and at the end of it I was happy to see my doctor and have him check the new X-rays. The bone had barely been cracked and I was a pretty fast healer. I was told to limit all motion, lifting, and the duration of use of my right arm. Still a pain in the ass but now I would be able to work again. The gunsmithing side of my life had a few jobs piling up waiting for me to heal.

Also, with my arm back, I'd be able to start planning my return to the hunt. I called Buntline. The circus had disappeared, gone from the state at the very least but neither hide nor hair of it could be found in the surrounding area. Unless it had gone north into Canada, where, he admitted, his connections thinned considerably.

My heart fell. I think in the back of my mind I had always assumed that Ian would find the circus, but it would be too far away for him to do anything legal about it. Then I'd get the address and go back on the hunt. But the damn thing had simply vanished into the air, or Canada.

Skylar's website was down, gone, no blog, but a sign saying it was under construction and coming back after the tour. Part of me worried that something might have happened to the girl. What if I had used her name and targeted her for God knows what? The rational part of my mind dismissed that. The clown was the problem, and he hadn't been present when I mentioned her. The thugs had beaten me up to protect the circus. They looked out for one another. Also to be noted, Ben had mentioned *they* were world famous. It was an entire family of multi-jointed people.

The case was firmly back on my shoulders. I was starting to have nightmares about the clown and his deep purple, bruised-looking skin. The more I had the nightmares, the more I felt that he wasn't even human. I knew that made no sense, but I couldn't shake it. Maybe he was a *freak*, born with a huge birthmark that covered his face in a purple blotch. It had to be rare.

I hit the computer hard. As I've said, my Google-Fu was weak. I searched for purple skin, skin deformities, famous side show freaks, and in a fit I even typed in Purple People Eater, but I all got was the song.

I gave up on birth defects and started typing in random strings of words. Searching for monsters in mythology, literature, and hell, even video games. I spent an entire day and night looking for any reference and I began to compile whatever data, no matter how far-fetched, I could find.

Who knew that a crazy, thirty-hour marathon search would change my life? As it turned out, it was the final nail in the new coffin that contained my life. As I said before, my search of a few weeks ago had triggered a hidden program, it had created a file in a bunker with my name on it. That file sat in a holding area for possible future issues. It only had a single warning flag on it. My thirty hours of searching hit all the criteria to fly past the second warning and put me right to the day's top priority.

My computer's firewall went down in a blaze and my anti-virus was tucked into bed and told to take a little nap. Of course, I didn't know any of that. I was banging my head against the desk and trying to figure out my next move when my computer chimed.

My computer had never *chimed* before and I looked up. A new icon sat in the center of my screen. It was folder simply labeled: *Hello Mr. Shaw.*

I stared at the icon and wondered how it had appeared. My computer chimed again and my hand hesitated on the mouse. What would happen if I opened the file? I had visions of nasty viruses tearing through my programs and ruining my businesses. Just what I needed to add to my frustration. I brought the mouse over the new file and right-clicked.

I said, "Fuck you, Mr. Hacker." I stared, dumbfounded, no properties list, no options, and no delete button came up. Apparently Mr. Hacker was very good. Besides the fact that the icon had appeared without opening a single email or even triggering my anti-virus.

I moved the pointer over my anti-virus icon and double-clicked. The window opened, but instead of the normal user interface all I got was a message: *Sorry, temporarily out of service. Please be calm, Mr. Shaw. I* am *hacking your system but all will be returned to normal. I believe I might be of some assistance to you. Please open the folder, your system will not be harmed.*

I saw that the light on my webcam was activated and I fought the urge to block the lens. Whoever this guy was, he was better than good, he was scary. I pretty much had two options: go along with him or pull the plug on my computer. Considering how bad things had already gone for me, I was beginning to think that it might be a good idea to have friends. So I opened the folder.

I turned and faced the camera. "Ok, you got my attention. Are you watching me? Listening to me?"

The only answer I got was another chime sound. The window opened and revealed several new icons. One was a Word file labeled simply: *Read First*. The rest had labels that drew my attention sharply. *Shaw, Henry Holmes Circus, Myths of the Far East, Itineraries of the Pattern,* and *Purple People Eaters.* I assumed that last one was a joke and it proved that I'd been under surveillance for a while.

I stared at the files. My fingers itched to open them all, but I finally followed direction and opened the word file. It was a letter:

> *Mr. Shaw,*
>
> *I'm here to help you. I've been monitoring your searches and though sloppy, they hit some alarm bells. I believe we can help. I understand it's hard to trust. I am the author of a program that monitors searches for the strange and unusual. A blog about a crypto zoologist discovering more proof about the Chupracabra — it went into the file. A story where a man claims a vampire or ghoul killed his friend? Into the file. A military unit disappearing on a peaceful mission, only their*

weapons found, empty? Into the file. The file grew, patterns emerged, and I and some like-minded friends formed a task-force. Now that taskforce is offering you a hand.

Our organization is small and we like to offer a helping hand, or a nudge here and there to help people to help themselves. In looking through your searches I have found a disturbing pattern. I'm sure you would have discovered it eventually. You will find a history and background for the Henry Holmes Circus within one of the files. I have also included a collection of myths that might have some bearing on your investigation. Your searches were fairly erratic and with more detail I might be able to furnish you with better results.

It's up to you on how to proceed. You can run with what I've given you or if you wish further assistance, it can be arranged. I will admit that I'm intrigued, as is one of my colleagues. The ball is in your court Mr. Shaw. In case you are having second thoughts or thinking this is some grand hoax I would direct you to the file marked with your name.

M—

There was an email address at the bottom of the letter. I leaned back in my chair and mulled it all over. I had no problem with accepting help. They were monitoring my searches? I wondered just who I was dealing with, and how far one could bend the Patriot Act. I pushed those thoughts aside.

I pushed the mouse over the file with my name and paused. What would I find? What could he possibly send that would convince me this wasn't some grand joke? Nothing ventured, nothing gained, I double-clicked icon and immediately a cascade of files opened. Window after window flashed by and as each opened I felt my guts twisting more and more. My tax returns, my licensing, my medical records, and even my high school transcripts flowed across the screen. They had my life in there.

I thought about it for all of a second. It was a pretty strange way to make friendly contact, but considering this guy could be anywhere in the world, it was the easiest method. Also I had to admit that taking charge of my computer was more impressive and far more likely to hold my attention. It didn't take me long to open my email and start typing.

I wrote my experiences with as much detail as possible. Strength, build, and speed of the clown. The exact shade of the purple skin, Barney Purple. The glowing red eyes and the flesh that resisted blows like solid stone. I even went so far as to try and describe the thing's voice. While writing it all, I could no longer call the clown a man. I finished the email, read it twice, and then hit the send button.

I don't know what I expected. But I sat there staring at the screen for a full ten minutes before I finally realized that the mystery hacker wasn't going to just instantly write me back. I stood, stretched, and then went to fetch a beer.

I went back to work while waiting for my mail to arrive. The very first thing I did as I sat back at my desk was open the Circus folder.

A slow, steady stream of information passed across the screen. The Henry Holmes Circus was an odd organization. It had existed for decades and had a larger presence in Europe, but had crossed the United States many times, especially in the last decade. The pattern of the crossing was what was strange. The show's presence was more pronounced in some areas of the States. The circus would show up in five to seven locations with performances spanning a few weeks in each, then would simply disappear for months or even a year before returning without warning to the same five to seven locations.

Over the entire last decade it had only appeared in the same small number of states: Connecticut, New York, Tennessee, Alabama, New Mexico, Southern California, Texas, Iowa, Indiana, Florida, North Carolina, and Georgia. Two years earlier, the schedule had been: June—Connecticut for three weeks outside Hartford; New York, Albany—two weeks; Rochester—three weeks; Poughkeepsie--two weeks. Then nothing for ten weeks, and then it reappeared in Tennessee, two locations total of five weeks, and then North Carolina in three locations for another six weeks. Then the show disappeared for two months before performing in Florida, Georgia, and Alabama. I couldn't imagine the entire circus just sitting idle for weeks at a time. Sure the acts would need some down time, but ten weeks between New York and the reappearance in Tennessee seemed a bit much. This area was marked with a note in red text that referenced the other file: *Itineraries of the Pattern.*

I opened that file and was astonished with the information within. Maps and patterns across the states and all in color-coded dots. Red dots marked the Henry Holmes Circus, Blue marked a "Fish Brother's Carnival", Green marked "Circe de Outre", and so on. Over a dozen different sideshows, freak shows, carnivals, and what have you.

Glancing through the rest of the files, I was overwhelmed with information. Each of the troupes was rated on the likelihood that they were an alternate name for Holmes' and his circus. There was a ton of raw data to pour through and I settled in. It was going to take a while.

I was an hour into the files when my computer made another sound. This time it was only my email. A thrill went through me and I rushed to open the letter.

Shaw,

Have conferred with colleague. Interest in case has expanded. Am sending a care package. In one week you'll have help. Good hunting.

M—

15

It was two weeks, not one, before I heard anything. They were weeks I used to work out my shoulder and get back into fighting shape. My broken nose healed well, without distorting my features. Not that the nose would have mattered when you looked at the scar snarling my cheek. It was still livid and red. The scab had long since washed away, leaving my skin pulled and twisted and the individual teeth marks obvious to anyone who cared to look.

Some mornings I hated looking in the mirror. I'm not a vain man. Ok, maybe I'm a little vain, but it seemed like that was behind me, or at the least tempered. I thought about growing a beard but that would only obscure the lower half of the scar and besides, my beard never came in full. I was anxious for news about the circus.

Part of me was still stressed and guilty that the clown was free. That Tommy's mother still lived in hope of finding her son with her ex-husband. Erin was a shadow of the woman who had approached me.

To add to my load I had also begun to talk to Ana Rook and I was beginning to think there might be something there. I never claimed to be the smartest man and when you added women to the equation…well you get the picture. My emotions were all tangled.

I was at my desk contemplating the whole dilemma, including the fact that I had no other PI work. Carpenter had been my first and only case. If not for investments and gun work, I would be in trouble. As it was, I had to watch my budget.

The bell rang. I figured it was the UPS man, since anyone else usually stepped into my foyer—I liked to call it a lobby but knew that term was too grandiose for the space—and rang the door to whichever business they were trying to find. They were usually looking for the gun shop.

I glanced at the monitor and saw a man with grey hair, carrying two bags, who was turned away from the camera. I stared for a few seconds, considered letting him walk away, and then thought better of it. I'd been told to expect someone—maybe this was it. I rose and hurried to the door.

I pulled open the door and blinked. I don't know what I expected, but this guy wasn't it. He looked like one of my professors. Grey hair neatly combed, grey eyes twinkling in mirth, and a pipe hanging from the corner of his mouth. He had on a tweed jacket with the leather patches on the elbows and a vest that appeared to have some chalk on it. He carried two large cloth satchels, old-style suitcases. He lowered the right hand one and held out his hand.

"Mr. Shaw, I presume?" he had a very slight accent that my brain registered as either Welsh or maybe Irish. A world of difference to be sure, but it was hard to place and I was still somewhat dumbstruck. It took me a few seconds to take the proffered hand. He grinned around the stem of his pipe.

As I let his hand go he pulled the pipe from his mouth and gestured to the Hunter poster in my window. "I have the same khaki's and pith helmet. Just lovely."

"Thanks." I didn't know what else to say and I'm sure he thought I was a complete idiot, but hey, these guys had me off my game.

He blinked, "Ha! Let me guess, you weren't clear on who was arriving?" He reached for his bag and I waved him off, taking hold of the handle for him. I was surprised at the heft of the bag and hid my frown as I dragged it into the foyer. "Thanks, lad. Yeah, it was down to Isabella or myself and since she was in Europe and I was closer, here I am, my boy. Mack has told me you have something special for me."

"Mack?" I said softly. So, my computer hacker had a name.

The old guy made no further comments as we stepped through the armored foyer and into my office. I placed his bag down on a low table and gestured around the room, "Make yourself comfortable...er?"

"My manners. Sorry. Bullfinch, Geoffrey Bullfinch. I hold degrees in Mythology and History. I lecture on the Occult and Cryptozoology and I try to find the bridges between Fact and Fiction. By the way, that is a lovely *Tosei gusoku,* a replica, I take it?" Bullfinch walked over to the suit of armor and looked it over.

"Yeah, it's modern, but it's completely handmade and based off an original, historical suit. I guess your historical studies include arms and armor?" I watched Bullfinch in a new light. He had disarmed me with his bookish looks, his trim build and grey hair. He moved with grace and I wouldn't be surprised to discover that he knew the martial arts. I'd be more surprised to find he *wasn't* a black belt in at least one of the arts. I was warming to this strange fellow already.

"I have made a study of many things and I find that the militant often dictate the course of history. As the old saying goes, the victor writes the history. How he won is as important to me as to any other part of the story." Bullfinch turned away from my martial arts wall and finally looked me directly in the face. He stared at the scar for a moment and then eyed me from head to toe. He nodded, as if satisfied by what he saw.

"I don't know what your trip was like, or from where, but I was thinking of making some lunch," I said. "Could I interest you in something?" I walked back into the kitchen and he followed as far as the doorway. I looked over my nearly barren shelves and the fridge was mostly full of beer and some leftovers.

"Tell you what," he said. "Put on some tea and I'll order out. There is an Indian restaurant not far from here that should make an exception and deliver for me." Bullfinch pulled a cell phone out of a pocket of his vest and I put the kettle on. He spoke into the phone in a mixture of English and Punjab.

I was impressed with his ability to speak their language. I put teabags into cups and then poured the water on and carried all into the office. Bullfinch closed his phone and sat across from me. He fiddled with his tea and we sat in silence for several minutes before he finally sighed and relaxed.

"We have much to go over and I hope you've been going through the files."

I nodded, "There was a lot of information going back decades, but I've been reading through most of it. To be honest, I think I'm overloaded. Wondering at different names and then going through all these different myths. There just seems to be too much to sort out."

We lapsed into another few minutes of silence and I opened the files on my computer to show him what I meant. When there was the sound of the doorbell. The food had arrived.

Bullfinch had ordered a large array of food and it covered my desk in various paper containers. We set too and ate for a while and then through some silent signal we both started talking about the issue at hand. I'd been waiting for two weeks to get back on the trail. A month overall since I'd been discharged from the hospital and I wanted another crack at the clown.

I had a whiteboard set up and I uncovered it as we ate. It had a list of the pertinent bullet points. Every detail I had been able to dredge from my memory. I even had a paint chip sample that was as close to the color purple as I could find, or as close as my memory would allow.

Bullfinch eyed the board and continued to eat. Then he paused. He looked down at the food and then back up to the board. He shook his head and I watched him, curious.

"Truly in mysterious ways," was all he muttered. "Fate is with us, lad." He put down his curry and then opened the bag I had carried in for him. He started to pull out several very thick tomes. No wonder it had weighed so much. He carefully set aside the first three books and then smiled as he pulled out a fourth.

"I believe we are dealing with an Asura. Ironic that we're eating Indian food. The Asura is a creature of Indian myth. Mysterious ways indeed." He flipped through several pages and glancing across the desk full of food, I saw that the book was handwritten and probably old as all hell.

"What's an Asura?" I put my food down.

"Well, it depends on whether you read Vedic or Buddhist stories, but the Asura is, basically, a minor god. A Christian calls it a demon. You have Deva and Asura, good and evil, though that is not strictly true. Again, we're talking a huge culture and reinterpretation and all of that. For example, in one legend they say that the Rakshasa is another name for Asura. While in another scripture, a Rakshasa is just a single type of Asura. Maybe not a big difference but still an important one."

I was getting what he was saying but at the same time I felt like I was floating above the chair and desk. The words *minor god* kept playing in my head, and *demon*. I think a part of me hadn't actually believed in my mysterious benefactor. I believe I really did think it was a huge prank, right up until Professor Bullfinch showed up at my doorstep. A learned professor matter-of-factly stating that I might have had a fight with an Indian demon, or minor god. Any other place I had this conversation and it would have been about a game or movie or TV show, or something other than real life. If the conversation *was* about real life, someone would have had you committed.

"Still with me?" Bullfinch pushed his food across the desk and put the tome on the top. He fiddled with his pipe. I realized I had spaced out in my thoughts for so long that I had missed some of what he was saying.

I sank back into the chair feeling the discomfort of the hot peppers burning in my chest. Maybe I hadn't been hallucinating that floating free of my body? Maybe these peppers had really kicked me into an out-of-body experience. I rubbed my chest and then stood.

"Excuse me for one moment, I just need a drink." I ignored the hot tea on the desk and went into the kitchen. Bullfinch gave a sly look. He had placed a bomb in the midst of relatively safe foods.

I took a chug of the milk bottle in the fridge and then grabbed a handful of Guinness's then headed back to the desk. I placed all three bottles on my side of the desk and opened one. I chugged half the bottle and then nodded, "Please proceed to tell me about the god who bit my face."

Bullfinch smiled and then tapped the page before him. "In the *Ramayana*, Rama fights against Ravanna, King of the Rakshasa. During the Siege of Lanka, there were Rakshasa that betrayed Ravanna and when he was slain by Rama he uttered a death-curse. The curse wasn't directed at Rama but at the Rakshasa that had turned against him. Now, this book was written by an Englishman who was in Japan when he wrote it, so the stories are all second hand through the Japanese. 'and these *rasetsuten*'—that's the Japanese for Rakshasa—'were cursed by their lord, the Godking Ravanna, who said they should live forever in torment, with all their many years weighing upon their flesh. To mark them, he turned their ebon flesh to the hue of deep purple', which in Japan and other parts of East Asia is the color of death." He paused and looked at me.

"So they were cursed with something and then marked with purple skin to further ostracize them?" I said. "Is there anything more on this curse?" I tried to think it through in my mind, assuming this was all fact instead of a legend. There had been a handful of soldiers who opened the back door and let a force into the castle. These soldiers were then cursed and marked with a purple stigma so everyone would know them for their betrayal. How does one live with the stigma? I tried to work out someone surviving through those past times. The clown in the modern era sort of made sense. You wore makeup a lot and if you lived in a circus that had actual—I hate using this word—freaks—where you could pass the purple off as a birth defect, or refuse to appear out of makeup. Bullfinch continued.

"The text goes on for pages talking about these particular Rakshasa. It even names them differently. They are called the Koshii. The curse, as you put it, is interesting and rather inventive. Koshii are immortal; all of the Asura are immortal. Immortal as in that they never age, but not that they cannot die. What Ravanna did was make the Koshii age. So they're immortal but they are still aging, growing older and more wizened with time."

"Yeah, well, I must have fought a really young one then, 'cause he was fast and built. No old guy with a walker for me. Plus his face was smooth and young. Believe me, I had my hands right in it."

"Yes, well, other texts go into details about that as well." Bullfinch pulled out a slim sheaf of pages held in a leather folio and tied with a silk ribbon. He untied and then opened the folio to reveal ancient, nearly translucent sheets of parchment or maybe vellum. He flipped through several of them, handling each one very carefully but with speed and assurance. He held up a sheet halfway through the stack. "Here we go. 'The Koshii is a ruthless beast with a hunger for the life and youth of humans. A Koshii is always much stronger and faster than a normal man. Even in the most advanced of ages, it will still be a dangerous foe. But the Koshii cheats anyway; it can devour the flesh of a human and thus restore its own youth and vitality. The younger the human, the more years the Koshii exchanges. Some Koshii have retained a grip on their Rakshasa roots and have the ability to create illusions or manipulate the senses of those around them. The Koshii has blessed skin, as do all Asura, making it armored against attacks of all but the most puissant of weapons. Extremely hard blows have been known to slow a Koshii if one is capable of delivering them to a joint or the eyes. Fire will slow them as it seems to cause them immense discomfort and perhaps they even fear it. The Koshii have a single bane and that is the wood of the Ash Tree. Impervious to all other weapons, a branch of Ash treats their flesh as if it were the merest tissue paper. A Koshii pierced through the body with a spear of Ash will become paralyzed. In this paralyzed state the creature will burn with but a touch of flame.'"

I blinked, "Well that seems pretty straight forward. Who wrote all that? I always thought research was a hard work."

Bullfinch stared at me for a moment and then pursed his lips. "It took me two weeks to get here because I already did most of the research. That bag of books represents about fifty different things that your *clown* could be. Research is a lengthy process, but it's my strong suit. Also, I didn't think you'd have too extensive of a library on antiquities, mythology, or folklore."

I held up my hands, "Hey, no offense intended. I prefer it this way. We have an idea of what it is and now we can get ready for it. Now we just need to find it. Speaking of which, with him eating all these people, don't you think it would leave a much clearer trail? I mean, you would think the circus would have issues with lots of missing kids everywhere." I glanced at my computer and the file about Far Eastern myths. I hadn't remembered seeing the Koshii within.

Bullfinch stood and paced the room, his eyes roving the walls and taking in the details of the room. He mulled over my questions.

"One would assume that he would only have to eat when he wanted. At least eat as in devour people. The book is quite clear that he exchanges years of life, and that children gave the most life, not that he had to eat them exclusively. I would imagine that he's fed off all sorts including the homeless and the *lost*, people that weren't missed. If he only kills one person a decade, it would be pretty hard to notice the pattern, especially since he travels the world." He began to pace again.

He moved from the replica armor to the kendo pads to the whiteboard. I picked up one of the translucent sheets of unknown material. It felt kind of stiff, but still had some flex, and the letters seemed almost etched into the surface. I was surprised to find the symbol of the Jesuits stamped into each of the pages.

"Be careful with those pages," Bullfinch said, glancing over at me. "They're from the late sixteenth century, the journal of a missionary Jesuit turned hunter of the Dark. His mind was apparently a million miles away, but he was still focused enough to be protective of his materials."

The documents were written in what I presumed to be archaic Latin. I really didn't know what to expect and wasn't surprised that I couldn't read the words. My face itched as I handled the page and frowned. The spicy foods were wreaking havoc with my system.

Bullfinch stopped his pacing to eye my collection of martial arts weapons. He began to nod slowly. He pointed. "The Jo sticks?"

I could hear the question in his voice and it took a moment for the gears to engage, but an answer surfaced. "Oak, not Ash. The bokken are layered bamboo so also not Ash."

"Yes, but if we had Jo sticks made of Ash, you would be… formidable?" He looked me over and I could see frank appraisal in his eyes. I stood to my full height, a hand over six feet and squared my shoulders.

I walked over to the display and pulled out the fifty-inch short staves—Jo sticks. “Quite formidable,” I said.

Bullfinch gave me room and I began working out the kinks, loosening my neck with a loud snap and shaking out my arms. My shoulder was tight but I worked into the katas, putting my body through motions ingrained over years of study. The staves sped up, whistling about my body and for the first time in a month, I began to feel whole again. The rage that always simmered beneath my surface was channeled into my hands and the staves. The room wasn’t large enough for me to really let it all out, but I worked up a slight sweat and was happy by the end of my chain of kata.

“I’m Sixth Dan, nearly twenty years of study.”

Bullfinch nodded and turned away from me, walking back to my desk. I didn’t know if I had impressed him or not but he seemed pleased. He gathered the journal and placed it back into the leather folio, then looked back at me. A smile played across his features. “We need to get our hands on some Ash Jo sticks.”

“We?” I settled back into my chair and Bullfinch eyed me again, his eyes narrowing to slits.

“Yes *we*. What did you think, that I was only here to do the research? Be glad it was I who got here and not Isabella, she would have left you in the dust and in the dark. I’m an academic, but I’m no stranger to the hunt. Dismiss the notion of doing this alone and start to think about where we can get our hands on some Ash.” He packed his books back into the satchel and I thought about what was in the other bag. I also wondered why I could never focus. I always had to wander around and then… epiphany.

I shot out of my chair, startling Bullfinch and threw my car keys into the air, snatching them as they dropped back down. “Want to come for the ride? I know exactly where we can get the Ash.” My grin made my cheek ache but I ignored it.

Bullfinch nodded.

I led the way, and as he followed, Bullfinch pulled out his phone, dialed, and started talking fast and low. I couldn’t hear what he said, but I assumed he was checking in. I wondered if he was giving me a passing grade.

16

I was impressed that Bullfinch didn't complain about my driv-ing. I usually went too fast, took corners too recklessly, or paid too much attention to my phone for most of my passengers. Wimps. I wondered if perhaps he lived a life like James Bond. Maybe he was used to car chases and jumping out of planes and people shooting at him.

For all I knew, the whole academic thing could be a cover. He could be straight up MI6. Hell, Bond's cover was as an International Businessmen. I almost missed the turn into the parking lot and the car skidded as I slammed the brakes, then fishtailed into the lot. It had rained earlier and the ground was still wet. I cursed softly and wished once again I had had the patience to wait for the dealer to find me a car with a standard transmission. I hated automatics and this was the first and last I would buy. It also occurred to me that if I just paid more attention to what I was doing, I wouldn't *need* the stick. Though thinking about it, I never would have been able to drive myself back from New York if I had a stick.

I slid into a parking space and looked around the lot. There was barely a soul in sight. I grinned at Bullfinch. For the first time in the entire trip he showed some emotion and he muttered something as he got out of the car, the only word I caught was Rebecca. I didn't ask.

I rounded the car and, with a flourish of my hands, I gestured to the entrance of the sporting goods store. He looked at me for a second and then slowly nodded.

Baseball. America's national sport and one I had been good at playing as a child. My father had hoped I'd go far with it, but Aikido and Rifle Team had been the stronger draws. I had no time for five AM Saturday morning baseball practice. Still, I'd learned a few things, and one of the few things I retained from my Little League years was instant recognition of the different styles of mitts, the positions for which they were intended, and the fact that the primary wood for bats was Ash.

I whistled as I entered the store and wandered through the aisles.

"The bats are on the back wall," Bullfinch said, catching on instantly. He pointed at a diagram of the store.

"Yeah, I've been here. But I like to wander, it helps me to think and besides, we might need some other supplies." I stopped before an aisle full of pads and pointed to the cups. "Sucks getting kicked in the balls and when facing a creature that is double your strength...." A salesman stopped midstride and then turned ninety degrees and walked over to a display, pointedly ignoring me. I sighed, because you never knew who was listening. I grabbed the jockstrap and looked back at Bullfinch. "Want one too?"

He shook his head, "No, I'm quite alright, thank you."

"You think I could get away with wearing skate pads?" I was looking at the knee and elbow pads. I couldn't imagine walking around all day wearing them "just in case." But if we got a tip and I went after the clown, the Koshii, then maybe I could get all *commando'ed* out: black tactical clothes, knee and elbow pads, my baseball bats. Yeah, the image made me laugh too.

I walked past the pads and down the aisle toward the back wall and the bats. I snagged a pair of MMA gloves off an end cap. They had the fingers bare and a few ounces of padding over the knuckles. I had some lead at home that would fit quite nicely into the knuckles. I would need the advantage.

There were so many bats. A lot of players had signature models and I tried to ignore these as most of them were made out of other types of wood. I started to grow grim as I noticed that the majority of the wall was covered in maple and newer bamboo bats. Things had changed in the eighteen years since I'd quit baseball. Bullfinch cleared his throat and I turned. He had two bats in hand.

"White ash, perfect for what we need," he said.

"Excellent, grab two more." He raised an eyebrow. "I have a few ideas and if you're coming along I want us both well armed."

Bullfinch smiled and reached for two more bats.

The salesman from earlier was manning the register and he gave me a funny look as we stepped up. I could only imagine what was going through his head. Two guys, one in his twenties and the other at least in his fifties, could be father and son. Buying four baseball bats, a jock and cup, and MMA padded gloves. I was almost tempted to ask him if they carried chaps just to see the look on his face. But I repressed the urge and paid with cash.

Once we stepped out into the parking lot I burst out in laughter. I lost it for a good minute, all the way back to the car. I popped the trunk and tossed our purchases inside. Bullfinch eyed the shotgun mounted to my trunk lid but didn't say a word until I closed the lid.

"What pray tell is so funny?"

"I was just imagining what that guy was thinking as he rang our sale. I have an idea that he thinks we'll be using them for something other than baseball." I gave him a significant look. It took a few moments to sink in and he shook his head in negation.

"Surely not..." he trailed off.

"People do some sick stuff." I grinned again and got into the car. He followed and once he had his seatbelt on I revved the engine, letting the tires spin on the wet pavement before pulling out of the lot and heading back toward the house.

17

We'd been driving for a full five minutes, at a much slower pace and without all the dramatics, when Bullfinch spoke up.

"Are we going somewhere else?"

"Nope."

"This isn't the path we took to the store." He watched the country slipping by.

"Like I said, I like to wander while I think. This is a slightly longer route but we'll get back just the same. It's got nice scenery." We passed a huge sprawling house. It was a large Tudor style with an even larger addition that was sheathed in field stone. It looked like a cottage attached to a castle. It was a house I always said I would try to buy if I ever struck it rich. I slowed as we passed it.

Bullfinch made some appreciative noises and I accelerated as it slid out of sight behind a swath of forest on the western edge of the property. I was tempted to turn on some music, but I had a feeling that our tastes would be worlds apart and I didn't want to shut out conversation. I tapped my fingers on the steering wheel, keeping the beat to one of my favorite songs as I tried to figure out how exactly I would find the circus. I knew Bullfinch's man on the net had dissected the pattern, but we'd already established that they didn't always get permits and he'd given me so many names that I still didn't know where to start. They didn't leave a credit card trail or much of anything really.

These people were nomads, actual Gypsies with no records, and no Social Security numbers. That got me. How the heck had the troupe come over from Europe and worked in America without going through customs? They had to. They had to have a visa to get into the country. Bands did it all the time in order to do tours. The circus had to be the same. I hadn't noticed if that was in the folder, but I was sure that if I was just getting the idea then they had figured it out far faster. What I needed to do was get the information into a more visual medium, either print it and spread it over the floor or maybe create a chart on my whiteboard.

I felt like a detective again—finally cutting away and finding the clues, putting the puzzle together. I tapped out a faster beat on the steering wheel, humming to myself and concentrating on the road. We went through a series of switchbacks and hills. I steadily accelerated through the entire series until we were being forced into our seats by the power of the turns. A cell phone was ringing and ringing and I made a glance at Bullfinch. He was gripping the "oh shit" handle and his seatbelt. He shook his head and I turned back to the road. It wasn't his phone.

We went into a sharp turn and angled down a hill. I let go of the wheel and grabbed my phone.

"Sweet Jesus, he's worse." Bullfinch was praying. I wondered if he was still talking about Rebecca, whoever that was.

I eased off the gas and put one of my hands back on the wheel as I thumbed the phone on and answered, "Hello, Shaw Investigates, Shaw speaking."

I tapped the brakes, slowed our descent and slid back onto our side of the road as a truck swerved around the corner. Bullfinch grunted. I flicked a glance toward him.

"Back to the road!" he yelled, closing his eyes.

I turned back to the road, catching the phone between my shoulder and my ear, and put both hands on the wheel. I missed the swerving truck by less than a foot and I hit the brakes harder and slowed down to twenty miles per hour as we came out of the hills.

The voice on the phone spoke again; I had apparently missed what it had said earlier. "Shaw! Are you there? Is this a bad time?" It was Ana Rook.

"What? No, it's ok now. How you doing Ana?"

"This is official, not social," she whispered the last two words and I imagined her sitting in a room surrounded by other cops. "Detective Buntline asked me to give you a call and tell you he might have some interesting information for you."

"Really?" I wondered if my luck was improving.

"Yeah. See, last year we had a different circus come through here. But it was kinda funny because it had two main tents and its main attraction was a 'Freak show in the tradition of the Old World.' The part you might find really interesting is that there was an article in the paper. We have a picture of the Ringmaster. Nice looking guy, trim and in an old style suit and with armless glasses. It was called the Fish Brothers Carnival."

My pulse quickened. The name triggered my memory. Fish Brothers was the first name on the list of possible covers. "Can you get me a copy of that picture? Fax or email it to me. Thank Buntline for me and thank you too, Ana. I owe you dinner."

She laughed into the phone, "Yeah, I'll get it faxed to you now. Be good and you better pay up." She made what sounded like a kiss noise into the phone and then hung up.

"You believe in fate… or perhaps a guardian angel?" Bullfinch had relaxed in his seat.

"I guess I would have to with the way you drive," he answered.

"I think we just got a lead on the circus. See what your guy can find when he searches for Fish Brothers Carnival. I know it was in his file, but see if they are billed anywhere currently." I grinned and gunned the engine again. I needed to get back and look at that picture.

"Funny. I'm not appreciating this circus sense of humor." Bullfinch paused and I glanced over. "Albert Fish was the name of another serial killer in the 20s. Little known fact his actual first name was Hamilton Howard, so making him another HH. He was a cannibal—and he ate children. I'm beginning to think this entire circus should be investigated. Mayhap your clown isn't the only evil hidden in its ranks."

I mulled over his words and tapped a little harder on the gas. I really wanted to get back on the road after the circus. I wanted the whole ordeal to be over. It was at that point that I fully realized the enormity of what I intended to do. I was going to hunt a creature down and kill it. I was literally hunting something that pretended to be a man. He would be protected by people who might not know any better, or worse, maybe they did know what he was.

In the movies, the heroes always hunt the monster, slay it, and live happily ever after. Maybe. Some movies were pretty dark and the hero didn't make it, but the point was they did the job, roll credits. I was going to kill and burn a Koshii. It would leave behind a skeleton, burnt fat, and other forensic evidence. Would a coroner be able to tell it wasn't human, or would it look like a normal man? Would I be arrested for murder? Would I have to fight and maybe seriously harm a bunch of misguided Gypsies? How would I get rid of the remains? Would Bullfinch and his pals back me?

So many thoughts. I wanted to reach for the radio again. I turned the corner and saw the house. Worries aside, I had a job to do. I had to see it through or I wouldn't be able to go on in any since of normalcy. The Koshii shouldn't exist in a sane world and I was a monster hunter.

18

Bullfinch followed me into the foyer and we took the right-side door instead of the left-side into my office. He followed without comment as we entered the gun store. It was a small shop, about half the size of my office; it was the same width but only half as deep.

The front area was filled with camping and hunting supplies, targets and general equipment. A glass case divided the front of the room from the rear third of the room and was double-locked and full of ammo and an assortment of pistols. Behind this counter the walls were covered in large, upright oak cases filled with rifles and shotguns that were also chained and double-locked in place. A single door interrupted the flow of rifles across the back wall.

I placed my bag and two of the bats on the glass counter and slipped around the side of the counter. I flipped a panel open beside the door and keyed in the code for my security system. I pulled a key from a chain on my belt and unlocked the door.

It opened into my inner sanctum: a secondary office and my full workshop. I have a computer in there with dual monitors and full access to all the information stored on the other computer and my security cameras. I flipped up a bank of switches and all the lights came on as the air conditioner turned over. I had removed the main windows from this room. Only thin-slit windows along the ceiling let in some light. The AC was needed to circulate the air and maintain a good temperature. The room was full of all the toys and tools needed for gunsmithing and most woodworking. A real cabinet maker or master carpenter would have thought it woefully inadequate, but a hobby woodworker and gunsmith would have been right at home.

The only access to my basement was also located in this room, and I had an extra bathroom and cot in the rear corner. The basement has a vault containing my overstock. I only have one of anything out front for the customers to peruse and as an added safety precaution most of the guns up front had their firing pins removed.

I'm not the neatest worker in the world. As if you couldn't image that by the way I ramble and do things, but I digress. I took the bats over to the main workbench and let Bullfinch take over the computer. He wanted to get into better contact with his people and have a look at the file already sent. Now that we had a name to focus on, everything was gaining momentum.

I eyed the bats as I had plans for them. We needed at least one of them to be sharpened down to a thrusting point and as much as I liked the idea of taking a full baseball swing into the bastard, I was thinking of trimming down the weight so that I could use one in each hand like a Jo stick.

I put the first bat into the lathe and worked it down to a smooth point using blades and then various grits of sandpaper. I had it down to a smooth polish when Bullfinch finally made a noise. He'd been silent for so long I will admit I had forgotten about the man. Luckily he didn't notice me start and nearly drop the finished bat.

"We have a few hits on the Fish Brother's Carnival. It is supposed to be on tour throughout Pennsylvania all next month. My people are running down the history of the Carnival, as best they can, to see if there are cities they favor. It seems to start in the Scranton area and since you disrupted them in New York, perhaps they've arrived early. I'll have more information in a bit," he reported.

I held the stabber up for him to look over. He lifted his head over the edge of the monitors and looked it over. He nodded his approval and then asked, "You going to fire-toughen that or leave it as-is? Also, I have had a thought: would you mind only taking some sandpaper down the length of my bat, nothing more? I'm wondering if the lacquer will interfere with the effect of the wood on the Koshii's flesh."

"Good points. I will run your bat through the belt sander and definitely fire up the spear. So you think you'll be ready for a road trip to Penn tomorrow?"

He glanced at the computer and then back at me. "I think I can be prepped and ready by tomorrow morning. I'm surprised that you're showing restraint. It suits you."

"Meh." I turned away from Bullfinch, hiding from the compliment. I really did want to get back in the car and head out. For once my paranoid side was winning out over my Aries "leap before you look mentality."

I took the gloss coat off one of the bats and then left it on the desk with Bullfinch. He ran a hand over the surface and nodded to me. Looking at the two screens I saw maps of Pennsylvania, scans of old flyers and permits, and the file with the *pattern.* I walked back to my bench and set to work on the last two bats.

The last two bats I merely thinned down with a blade on the lathe and a strip of sandpaper. I dropped each one down several ounces and then tested them. They whistled around as I did a few wrist turns. There wasn't enough room in the cluttered room for me to really let loose. Either way, they felt good in my hands. I sat back at my bench and glanced over at Bullfinch. He was deep in conversation with someone at the other end of a long fiber-optic cable, fingers hammering at the keys in a steady stream.

I grabbed a can off my bench top which contained an assortment of brass tacks and odd nails. I tapped a handful of them down the upper ends of each of the bats, just adding the studs for a little *flare.*

I pulled out the MMA gloves and loaded the knuckles with lead powder trying them out. It made my hands heavy but not so much that it would slow me down. I tried out the bats and felt my grip was still secure enough to make the gloves worthwhile. I contemplated adding a few tacks to the gloves and decided that it was going too far, plus I was getting bored with the projects. Boredom was my personal bane, it was the reason for so many degrees and so many odd jobs, and it had to be fought whenever it reared its head.

I grabbed a dustpan and a broom and started to clean up the curls of Ash under the lathe. When I was finished, I placed the dustpan on the workbench and turned to Bullfinch. He had his head down close to the desk and was carving sigils into the bat with a penknife, all the while muttering words under his breath.

"Hey Bull, you got a sec?"

He didn't respond until he finished his current carving and then it was only a grunt. I took that as an assent and continued.

"How did the report on the Koshii put it? Was it that the touch of Ash turned the skin to something like tissue paper?" He sighed and I wondered if perhaps that grunt hadn't been an okay to continue.

"I translated it as tissue, but technically it was stated as rice paper. I'm involved in a delicate task, Mr. Shaw. Perhaps if I went to the other office we'd both be better off?" He gathered his things and stood before I could respond and I shrugged.

I led him through the foyer and unlocked the door to my office. I apologized as I gestured him through. "Make yourself at home. The kitchen's open to you if you need tea or whatever. Sorry to interrupt your… carving. I think I have a little surprise in mind that I think you will like. If you get tired, there is a guest room at the top of the stairs, second door on the left."

"Thank you, and sorry… Jon. I just need to focus."

I left him in the office and headed back to my workshop. The pan full of Ash shavings sat on the counter and I grinned as my *surprise* took full shape in my mind's eye. I began to whistle as I walked about the room pulling down the supplies I would need. I reached under the reloading bench where I had pre-primed, but otherwise empty shotgun shells.

Powder, cup, 00 buck, and wood shavings and dust. The powder would burn up the dust, but it might still coat the buckshot and hopefully the wood curls would carry for at least a few yards. *Let's see him take a shot of 00 buckshot to the guts with his skin turned to tissue paper*, I thought.

I loaded twenty shells. If I needed more than that, I'd be dead or surrounded by the police. As it was, I would still have to worry about the police. I was getting jittery even though I had no real reason to be. Going into Pennsylvania might end up a total bust, and yet I felt like a kid on Christmas Eve.

I cleaned my shotgun, loaded it with some of the new shells and filled a pouch with the rest. I cleaned and prepped my Kimber and wished I had the supplies to make .45 shot shell for it as well. I resisted the urge to grab more guns, deciding they would be useless against the Koshii and probably only weigh me down. However, the eyes were vulnerable.

I grabbed a couple of cans of pepper spray and stuffed them into the bag as well. It should work on the Koshii and would be a good non-lethal way to handle the carnies if they got involved again.

I checked the clock. It was one in the morning and I'd done enough. I hit the bank of lights and decided to crash on the cot in my workshop. Hopefully Bullfinch felt relaxed enough to find his way to the guest room. Otherwise, he'd have to sleep on the love-seat in the office.

19

We hit the road early. Weapon bag on the backseat, bats hid-den under a blanket, and I won't tell you how uncomfortable it was driving while wearing a brand new cup.

We didn't drive for long. The first leg of our journey was to the Tower, Sentry Hill's best breakfast spot, bar none. I didn't know if fate would still be with me today, but there was a good possibility that I would find the circus and the Koshii. This might have been my last chance for a decent meal, so I took it. Scratch-made corned beef hash, an omelet, extra rye toast, and fried potatoes and I was in heaven.

Bullfinch mostly kept his eyes on his cell phone, scrolling through screens full of data. When I was nearing the end of my feast he began to talk.

"The troupe is scheduled to arrive in Scranton in about three weeks, then Gettysburg, and finally in Monroeville—at least by the original timeline. I would assume it would go through another name change and on into Ohio but there's no way to know that for certain." He slipped the phone into a breast pocket. He was still dressed as the academic, I had half-feared that his jokes about a pith helmet and English khakis had been true, but this morning he had been dressed similarly to yesterday, though I noted with quick respect that he wore nothing loose and no tie, rings, or jewelry. Everything was tucked and squared away while at the same time still conveying the image he wanted you to perceive. I was wearing a tucked-in T-shirt, very loose cargo pants—double belted—and a light coat that hid my shoulder rig.

"So we head directly for Scranton then and start looking for campgrounds and recreational parks in the area. It's pretty damn hard to hide that many trucks and campers." I drained my coffee and picked up the bill. I dropped a generous tip and headed for the door.

It was a three-hour drive to Scranton and we made good time, but I didn't go overboard. My usual lead foot was tempered by the bag with the shotgun sitting on the backseat and the bats that had been rendered into even more lethal weapons. I didn't want to get pulled over and test just how much pull Bullfinch actually had.

I pulled off of the highway as soon as the first exit for Scranton showed up and tapped my GPS as I pulled into a gas station. I had Bullfinch ask the GPS for the nearest truck stop and I went to pump the gas.

We were becoming a pretty good team and by the time I had finished pumping, he had a map to the nearest stop already calculated into the GPS. It was on the south end of the city and the route took me there fast.

It was a mom-and-pop-type place, not one of the huge chain-style truck stops. There was a huge, low wooden building that had gas lanes on either side of it. One side was for truckers and large RVs while the other side was smaller scale for passenger cars. The wooden structure in the middle was sprawling and the entrance looked like it might have been a transplanted Honky Tonk from the southwest. As we entered, the illusion strengthened. Pretty much everything a trucker or camper would need was located in this building. There were showers, a general store, a huge restaurant, and an enormous bar complete with dance floor and a mechanical bull in the corner.

I wanted to chuckle as we wandered through, but an assortment of hard drinkers was already lining the bar. A handful of them wore biker leathers. The restaurant was doing brisk business and we decided to sit and try out the menu. Yes, I was actually hungry again, despite my huge breakfast, and yes, I was going to take a chance at getting some more food.

We had already agreed that if we found the circus we would wait until night fall and try to approach the Koshii in stealth, so

I had no worries that I would get into a fight with a loaded gut. I ordered a burger and Bullfinch got the meatloaf as I attempted to chat up the waitress.

"You gentlemen care for some dessert?" she said. "We got the best strawberry rhubarb pie in the state." Her name was Jamie and she was seeing the end of thirty, but was still a trim and well-proportioned woman. She seemed to be taken with Bullfinch and he was a very charming gentlemen.

"Absolutely my dear, that would be superb, and more of the coffee if you please. Just one question, where would one find a good campground, something that takes RVs?" I smiled into my coffee cup. He was slick.

Jamie smiled. I think it was the accent that really had her. She refreshed his cup from her pot and ignored mine. She outlined directions to a campground up the way, even leaning into the table to draw a little map on Bullfinch's napkin. I couldn't help but notice that she leaned in such a way as to afford him a good view of her cleavage.

I edged in a question of my own, "Does it have easy access for, say, a rig with a fifty-two-foot trailer?"

Her nose wrinkled as she glared at me, "I'm not a trucker, how would I know? Ask one of them." She turned back to Bullfinch, her face smoothing back out and the smile returning.

Good idea, I thought. I left the booth.

The first driver I talked to was in no mood to talk to me, so I moved on. Luckily, my short stint in auto mechanics was spent changing tires on big rigs and dump trucks, so at least I knew some of the lingo. The next guy I talked to was an old driver and he liked the company. It only took me a few minutes to find out that the campground wouldn't allow a full rig through and that there were ways to tell an independent from a commercial driver. He gave me a few pointers, but it took another ten minutes for me extricate myself from the rambling conversation.

Bullfinch had eaten my slice of the pie by the time I got back to the table. I dropped a few bills and we headed toward the doors. There were maps of the area, including brochures for the local campgrounds right at the door and I rifled through them looking for anything useful. I stuffed the large pockets on my pants and froze as the stand began to shake.

A wave of thunder rolled up and I smiled. It was the roar of many V-twin engines: full-bore hogs pulling into the parking lot. Bullfinch was staring at the door and I felt drawn. I stuffed the last brochure into my pocket and stepped outside into the lot.

20

I stepped out and into a cloud of dust and the smell of hot chrome. A wind whipped the dust away from me and I felt Bullfinch stepping up to my back, but my gaze was locked forward. At least thirty bikers were arrayed before me. These were the real-deal road warriors: every bike was chopped, augmented, and lovingly tended. Each was a unique symbol of the man, or woman, riding it. Every single bike was laden with saddle bags and several had small bike trailers attached, one even had a sidecar that a young kid wearing goggles was climbing out of. He looking a little wobbly from the road. A van hauling a huge trailer also circled past the bikers and parked around the side of the building. It was a damn big group and with all the gear and a truck, I would have to guess they were moving to a new clubhouse.

Everyone, except the kid in the goggles, was sporting colors, either a jacket or vest covered in the Club insignia. One bike, a huge, decked-out Honda Goldwing, sported a massive standard, a blue field with a white cruciform sword, point down. These were the real-deal bikers. They looked like a mass of Vikings with their long hair and beards, and I swear, some of the men were even sporting horned helms. I cannot make this up. I wanted to pull out my phone and start snapping shots—mostly of their bikes, but definitely of the redhead with the six-pack abs and leather halter top that was pulling the kid out of the sidecar attached to her bike.

The side of my face started to itch and I slapped at it gently.

"Trying to wake yourself up? This is not a dream." Bullfinch stepped out from behind me, his eyes locked on the man I automatically assumed to be the leader. I assumed this mostly because he was centrally parked, but also because he had a sword similar to the one on the banner strapped to the sissy bar on his bike. I wondered what the legality of that was.

"No, my face itches and I don't want to scratch at the scar tissue," I matched his pace as we headed toward the bikes.

The leader turned and locked his gaze on Bullfinch, who stopped in mid-stride. The itch in my face intensified. I cursed and slapped my cheek, hard. I looked up; everyone in the lot was frozen. Most eyes were locked on Bullfinch, but a few were looking at the leader. I wondered if our approach had been taken as an insult. Then the leader laughed and shook his head, he was looking right at me and I wondered just how loud the slap had been.

"Geats to me, the rest of you eat and refresh." Two leather-clad men stepped behind the leader and the rest of the bikers turned away from us and headed toward the doors at our back. The accent was pure French.

"Geats?" I asked toward Bullfinch, attempting to shift my voice low.

"Very interesting," was his response.

I was startled by a third voice, "The Geat brothers, Wulf and Liam. My name is Roland." It was the boss man; he threw a thumb over each shoulder as he named each of the brothers. As we stepped forward to close the distance I eyed them.

Wulf and I stood eye to eye, but he had to have at least seventy pounds of raw tattooed muscle over me. He looked like Conan, with a mane of long black hair held back with a studded leather head band and his waist was wrapped with a length of heavy chain, the hilt of a heavy knife peeking out from beneath. He had a huge beard forked into two thick braids.

Liam was the same height and I would guess weighed as much as myself and while his brother was dark of hair and brutish of face, Liam was red-haired and clean-faced. He was untucking his shirt to hide a matching set of pistols on his hips. I recognized the marks on the grip.

"Kimber?" I flicked my jacket aside, showing off the shoulder rig and Liam smiled. Wulf snorted disapproval or contempt it was hard to say.

"We just wanted to admire your bikes," Bullfinch stepped wide around the trio and eyed Roland's bike. "I like the horses you have painted on the tank. *Veillantif*, that's an... interesting name."

I was lost at what was going on, but something was playing out between Bullfinch and Roland. The air was laden with hidden meaning. I knew that if it was just the Geat brothers and myself, we'd be hitting it off and bullshitting. But whatever was passing between Roland and Bullfinch had all of us in its grip.

"A noble steed for a noble man. Perhaps I take on airs, perhaps not." Roland smiled; it was hard not to like him. He was not the most imposing man out of the group, barely six feet tall and while his dark blond hair was long, it was in a neat braid and his beard was trimmed. It was his eyes and his *presence* that demanded attention. The eyes were a freakish bright blue.

"Yes, a very noble steed, with a history all its own. Perhaps you carry the Oliphant as well?" Bullfinch had a note in his voice, a shift in tone. Wulf's hand went to the knife on his belt and I tensed, but Roland's hand stopped Wulf.

"Indeed I do carry the horn. We are the Paladins and are new to this area. We're only passing through, looking for some good food and a place of rest, we already faced some resistance. No need for more trouble."

I jumped in because I didn't understand what was passing between the two of them, but I knew I didn't need trouble with anyone else. Plus, any band called the Paladins couldn't be all bad, even if they were a bunch of Viking-looking bastards. "We're just passing through ourselves, not local color at all, so there is nothing between us other than words and well wishes. You've had trouble and we're off to look for our own. The less said, the better. You have some nice rides."

"He's on the hunt." Wulf's voice was just as dark and brutal as the rest of him.

Roland turned his eyes on me and I felt the itch burn across my cheek again. "He's been marked." This from Liam. I hid a wince and began slapping my cheek again. "See."

Roland stepped right up to me and put his palm right over

the scar on my face. "Do you mind?" he asked, but didn't wait for an answer. The itch flared up and then faded away, changed and Roland closed his eyes. It felt pretty weird to have some strange guy touch me in such an intimate manner. I opened my mouth to speak.

Next thing I knew I was back in the woods, I was fighting the Koshii and things were not going well. The teeth were biting into my flesh again and I was scrambling to draw my gun. I was in full-on panic and just as suddenly as I was reliving the moment, I was back in the parking lot and Roland had moved his hand to my shoulder.

"A hard battle and to go so woefully unarmed, you have heart. You might do well under our banner, but our paths are divergent. When you're done you might want to look us up." Wulf grunted again and turned away.

"Thanks, I think."

"The circus you seek is a hundred miles south of here. We encountered them this morning; they made camp where we were departing. We've had past… dealings." Roland glanced over at Liam, "It looks like HH might have picked up another snake."

"Wait. You know about the circus? And, by the way, did you just read my mind?"

Roland laughed, "Your mind? No, I have not that gift, I merely read the pain of your wound and I saw the memory of that single moment. As to the circus, it has been around for a long time and is not all black."

"We call it the Damned Circus," Liam cut in. "Most of the people in it are poor bastards who wouldn't have a home otherwise. HH is always willing to offer sanctuary to those in need, especially those that meet his criteria. Once in a while a snake will sneak past him."

"Ok, time out. I'm willing to accept a lot of things but not pure chance that I would just step out into a fine August afternoon and the leader of a biker gang—"

"We prefer motorcycle club, or brotherhood."

I ignored the interruption and continued, "Just happens to know all about me and what I'm doing and you just happen to have the exact bit of information I need? Look I love luck, I believe in luck. Better lucky than good is one of my mottos. But paranoia and 'always carry a bigger stick' are also two of my personal beliefs. I just… I mean…." For once, my brain engaged before my mouth, I didn't want to say what I really thought. But Roland could read me anyway.

"You don't trust us. That is understandable. God is great and he does work in mysterious ways. I believe he has led me to this place, at this time, that I would give you the words you needed. You hunt a vile foe, and had we known of him, we would have dealt with it this morning. If we weren't already sworn to our own quest I would join you. The brotherhood would mount up and ride to your battle. We would earn your trust." He reached out and grasped my right forearm in a warrior's clasp, I grabbed his forearm and we locked together.

He looked into my eyes and I blinked. I suddenly found myself elsewhere, and else-when. I was floating above a rough track cutting through a mountain, a narrow pass that wouldn't be considered more than a hiking trail. Two men stood at the narrowest point of the pass. The way before and behind them was choked with the dead. Men and horses covered in armor and coats. I floated even closer and I saw one of the men looked like Roland, though he wore full-plate armor, battered with the hacks and hewing of many blades. His surcoat was slashed to ribbons, his helm lay discarded and dented at his feet and his single companion wasn't in any better shape.

Before them and down the slope was a sea of bodies, hundreds if not thousands of dead and dying men, and at the base of the rise an army waited. With a roar, a final wave of Calvary pushed up the slope. Dark-skinned and covered in robes and light armor, they waved scimitars in the air and screamed as they rode.

I was seeing a last stand, two French knights facing a sea of moors or Saracens. I didn't know my history well enough to place them. Suffice to say they were of Middle Eastern descent and they were about to wash over the final two knights and take the pass. The maybe-Roland pulled a horn from his back, a huge hollowed ram's horn chased in silver; he brought it to his lips and blew. A blast of sound, deafening and awe-inspiring blasted the mountain-side and the charge faltered. He blew a second time, staggering as the wave of sound literally knocked some of the riders from their mounts. The charge continued. A third blast of the horn, blood pouring from Roland's nose and ears, the knight threw the horn down and drew his sword and limped to meet the final wave.

I would have staggered, but Roland held my arm tightly as I came out of the vision.

"I swear on my name and the name of my horse, and by Christ the Redeemer that all I have spoken to you is true. The enemy you seek is a hundred miles south of here hidden among the ignorant, outside the township of York. If you ask, I will send one of my Brethren with you as guide and guardian."

I was taken by his formality and still shaken from the vision. I flicked a glance to Bullfinch. I couldn't read the man's expression but he gave a slight shake of his head. I didn't know which part he was negating, but I followed my gut.

"I believe you Roland, and don't think I'll ever ask for your word again. I trust you. I think we'll be fine on our quest and as you said, you're locked in your own, so I will refuse your guide, with thanks." He grinned and released my arm.

"Well, at the very least let me arm you with knowledge. HH is not a bad fellow, but he does get over-protective and occasionally he is blind to the sins of his followers. I'm sure you've met his men; he usually keeps a stock of thug workers who are more than willing to get their hands dirty. Again, most of them are not bad men but they are very… zealous in their duties.

"HH believes in creating a home, a haven for those who are deemed 'not normal' by society. The Damned Circus has existed for well over a century. I think HH claims his great-great-grandfather founded it in 1850. The occasional bad apple has been drawn to the circus—a criminal seeking asylum or to lose himself in the nomadic lifestyle of the troupe. Occasionally those twisted of body also suffer from perversions of the mind; it happens." Roland paced back and then sat on his bike, crossing his arms over his chest.

"Tell him about the werewolf," Liam chimed in. His brother grunted again and then walked into the restaurant.

"The werewolf?" I flicked a glance back at Bullfinch who was interested again.

Roland sighed and continued, "You know the actual definition of Lunacy?"

"Moon madness," Bullfinch said. "There were men and women who would literally go wild with the phases of the moon. Even today, police statistics show that more crimes happen during the night of a full moon."

"Right. The Circus had a man who was afflicted with a great amount of body hair. They called him the werewolf, and he was kept in a cage. He'd rattle the bars and they'd throw meat at him and the crowd would go nuts. This was the sixties and we—well, the previous members of the brotherhood as I was only two years old at the time—encountered the Circus in Hamburg. What no one realized about the *werewolf* act was that the man really believed he was a wolf. On nights of the full moon he went crazy. I don't know how he got out, but that's what happened. He got out, killed a couple of kids and then went into town. The brotherhood ran into him at a bar where he went berserk and killed another four people before finally being put down. HH was distraught and he tried to make amends. He paid families and made restitution and swore to not return to Hamburg for thirty years. That was our first encounter with HH."

I nodded, mulling over the story. I knew the clown was a real monster, not some maniac in thrall to the lunar cycle. Despite the visions and oddness displayed by Roland and his band, I wasn't ready to share that secret yet.

"Well, we have another maniac hiding in the circus. I don't know how much you got off that touch, but we have a clown that is killing kids. We're going to *stop* him." I made my idea of what "stop" meant with the set of my face and the tone of my voice. Roland nodded just once, he got it loud and clear.

"We've said it enough, but again, the circus will protect their own until shown a reason to do otherwise. Not everyone is your enemy. Fight wisely. Happy hunting." He shook Bullfinch's hand first, meeting the scholar's gaze for several seconds before breaking into a grin. He shook my hand, two quick pumps and then brushed past me to head toward the doors. I was happy to not have a vision at his touch.

I turned and called to them before they entered, "Where are you guys headed? What's the final stop?"

Liam answered, "Mass."

I nodded, "Well, you ever need anything, maybe a fix on those pistols or what have you, Shaw Firearms in Sentry Hill, Connecticut. Look me up."

"Connecticut? Interesting, thank you for the offer and a word of warning back to you. If you see any bikers whose colors are of a skull wearing a horned helm, with coins for eyes and a pair of crossed axes in the background, stay clear of them."

"Right. More Viking bikers, stay clear. Got it. Don't forget to try the strawberry rhubarb pie, I hear it's good." A glance to Bullfinch, who looked unashamed.

Liam waved and then mimed a pistol shot with his index finger. He and Roland swept through the doors into the Honky Tony Truck Stop. It would not be the last time I ran into the Paladins, but that's a different story.

Bullfinch didn't say a word until we got into the car.

"That was a very strange bunch," he said. "*Very.*" He didn't elaborate further.

"Yeah, I got that with the flags and strong Christian belief and all that. Still wouldn't want to get in their way. I could tell something was up between you and Roland, though." I pulled out of the lot after typing YORK, PA Center into my GPS.

Bullfinch snorted, "Roland? Do you have any idea who he's modeling himself after?"

"If you tell me a French knight who held a pass against thousands of Arab warriors I think I'll scream and drive us into a tree." He remained silent and I didn't want to look but I had to.

He stared right at me, his mouth slightly open and emotions warring in his eyes until finally he narrowed them, as if judging me.

"Stop that."

"I've seen how you drive; I don't want to hit a tree." He laughed. "But you are dead right. Roland was one of Charlemagne's Fellows, his *Paladins*, an Order of Holy Knights. It's a lofty role to assume."

I had a feeling that it wasn't just an assumed role. I had a feeling that the man we had just met was Roland reborn. When I got back from this hunt, I was really going to have to sit down and start trying to figure out just what was real again: what beliefs, myths, and fiction were really just aspects of a broader reality. I mentally checked off reincarnation as *likely*.

The Paladins were moving into Mass, what was going on there? Did I even want to know, and if Roland was reincarnated, what about the rest of the crew? Were they God's chosen, holy warriors disguised as a band of bikers?

Concentrating on the "what ifs" of the club wouldn't help me with my own battle, so I cleared my mind and hit the gas pedal. On to York.

21

Hours of travel later we sat at a rest stop looking over the maps and trying to figure just where the camp would be and how best to approach.

"Do you think they dusted off one of their names and are doing an impromptu show?" I didn't know how well-off the show was financially, but I imaged that weeks sitting in a camp without performing would have to be eating a ton of their money, even if they only set up the rides and games, maybe the secondary tent.

"If they have set up, then there will be flyers, or some form of advertising that would lead us to them."

He was right and I mulled it over. I think the real reason we were parked on the edge of the town was the reality of what I planned. We hadn't really spoken about it in detail and I was surprised at how readily Bullfinch had traveled with me. I glanced back at the bat handles peeking out of the duffle bag on the backseat.

"Are you in this all the way?" I finally asked after the silence had stretched for a full minute.

"What is *this*?" he asked back.

"You know… killing the Koshii. I mean, the only evidence we have is I saw purple skin under the paint. It really could be a strange birth defect."

"Mr. Shaw, are you forgetting that you emptied a gun into the Koshii, and that he got up again? I can understand being nervous that we might have the wrong creature, we did leap onto the first thing I found. But I am sure, based purely on your conviction and impassioned words, that we face a monster, a creature that should not exist in this world. I am wholly with you on this and the organization I'm a part of was not founded to capture and cage the dark, but to face it and repel, to protect the world and maintain balance. If this creature was in trouble, or needed help, that is what I would offer. If it needs to be destroyed...."

The words helped, but still I felt a coil in my guts. Perhaps it was just a bad case of nerves. "He could have been wearing a bulletproof vest." Even as I said the words I knew they were weak sauce.

Bullfinch snorted and looked me right in the eye. "Mr. Shaw, start the car and let's go into town. We have a job to do and I'm sure that if you think about it, you'll realize that the Koshii was not wearing a vest, or anything else under his makeup."

I put the car into drive and we drove into the town. It barely rated the name town, though it was a far larger place than my tiny little village in the hills. We drove past a huge cemetery, Prospect Hill, as we headed south on route 83. We came to the centre and discovered that York boasted two colleges, a branch of Penn State and York University.

We found lots of interesting stores, including a huge book store and several niche markets—a pleasant walk for a shopper. The area around the colleges was fairly nice and I parked the car in the middle of it all.

"We should go into the book store when we're finished." Bullfinch released his seatbelt and opened the door.

I stared after him and had to jump out of the car. He stretched and when he turned to me I asked, "You want to go shopping when we're finished?"

"I thought you might get upset if I suggested we waste time now doing it. I mean, you don't intend to hunt the Koshii until tonight, saying we find them."

I shook my head, "We'll find them. Roland said they were here and they'll be here." I punctuated my words by tapping my index finger unto the roof of the car. A trio of co-eds walked by and I perked up. "I'll ask the locals."

I trotted after the ladies and left Bullfinch doing his stretching. He looked like he belonged on the campus.

I caught up to the women, asking them if they knew anything about a circus coming to town. It probably wasn't the best ice-breaker but I can be charming when I want to, even with a mangled cheek. It was a short conversation, the gist of which was that no circus was in town and that there was a fairly large campground in the North West corner of York. If we hadn't followed 83 right into town, but had instead circled the whole of the city, we would have encountered the place; it was well north of our location and off a public park named Stillmeadow. I thanked the girls and headed back to the car.

Bullfinch had wandered off into the quad, but I had faith he'd be back. I pulled a map out of the car and spread it over the hood. I nearly cursed as I found the park and the campground marked on the map which we had passed within five miles of on our way there. I traced a route back to it and looked for a place I could park and enter the grounds.

Stillmeadow Church of the Nazarene looked as good a place as any. It was on the far corner of the area marked as "woods and campground," at least a quarter mile or more away from the camp proper, but all of what lay in between would be woods. I also had an idea my car wouldn't be towed if it was parked on the church lot.

I looked around for Bullfinch, but there was still no sign of him as I glanced over the groups of twenty-somethings walking around the campus. A truck caught my eye. An older model it was hauling up the street, a full twenty miles over the limit. I leaned against the hood of my car, putting as much space between myself and the speeding truck as possible.

I was raising my hand to flip off the driver when I met the eyes of the passenger. I had time to notice the piggish eyes widening in recognition as the bearded face blurred by. I was around the hood of my car and heading across the quad as brakes squealed and the pickup slewed to a stop. I ducked my head, trying to hide my height and to blend into a crowd of students. Where the hell was Bullfinch, and what were the odds that Lazlo would be riding in a truck through the center of the damn town?

I left the crowd, ducked behind a tree and took a glance back at my car. The truck had turned around and was slowly heading back up the street, both driver and passenger staring out across the quad.

I wondered just what I'd done to incur this karmic debt. I was trying to do a good deed here. I pulled out my phone and texted Bullfinch. The truck turned around at the corner and stopped long enough for Lazlo to get out. Then it slowly drove back up the street, barely creeping by when it reached my car. Then it hit the corner and took a right. I turned back to watch Lazlo's progress and was startled that I had lost the man.

How the heck do you lose a near seven-foot bearded brute?

I started to text again when a voice spoke at me back.

"What are you doing, Jon?" Yeah, I will admit I nearly screamed and jumped up the tree. Bullfinch had found me and was frowning at his phone.

"Where the heck were you?" I whispered. I scanned the crowd again and spotted Lazlo moving around a tree and walking along the side of one of the buildings. If he continued on his path he would be deep into the campus and we'd be able to get back to my car.

"I was looking around the campus. The circus is not set up anywhere, or if it is they certainly haven't tried to advertise here. What are you doing?"

"Lazlo. Carnie drove by in a truck and now he's hunting across the quad for me. What the hell are the odds?" Lazlo passed beyond sight around the back of the building and I turned back to the car. The truck was still gone, perhaps going around the entire block. I didn't really care. "Come on, he just went out of sight."

I ran for the car, not checking to see if Bullfinch was with me. I slid across the hood in my best T. J. Hooker impression and whipped the door open, diving into the driver seat. I glanced up and was pleased to see that Bullfinch had kept up. He dropped into the car, a little color on his cheeks.

I reversed out of the spot faster than I should have and took off down the street. A horn blared at me and I ignored it. Better to have someone calling me names than to have the damn carnies after me. They would ruin things. I had an idea that Lazlo wasn't the type to listen to reason. He wouldn't believe my *bad seed* story and his only answer would be ham hock fists. If Ben was around I might be able to appeal to his sense of reason. He hadn't taken part in the beating, but he hadn't stopped it either.

I cursed as I realized I had left the map on the hood of the car. It was long lost now and I tried to remember the route I had traced. I wracked my brain for the names of streets and the general path, but the only thing that came up was the name of the park and that it was north of where I was currently.

I finally calmed enough to get my mind back in order and pulled into a gas station. I sat at the pump for a full minute before I moved for the door. Bullfinch stopped me.

"Are you going to be alright, Jon?" He gripped my arm and I took a deep breath. My body had gone into full-flight mode and now that I was sitting at the station I felt foolish.

"Yeah, I guess I just went into panic mode. I mean, what are the chances that he really recognized me? I just don't want this thing ruined. I'm not looking to battle through a bunch of carnies who mostly think they're doing a good thing. They don't know they're protecting a cannibal monster." I opened the door and stepped out, paused, then leaned back into the car, "At least I hope they don't know they're protecting a cannibal."

I went into the mini-mart, grabbed a new map and a couple of sodas, then headed back to the car. I was already opening the map and looking for the park, so I failed to notice the pickup truck two blocks away, idling.

I got into my car, holding up the map and pushing a cola toward Bullfinch. I highlighted the map, including a few extra routes that would take us around the park and the campgrounds. I wanted to do a drive up around the area looking for the semi trucks as they would be the last thing to leave and if I found them, then I would be certain that the rest of the troupe was there.

I took off from the station. The truck followed once a few other cars got behind me. I'm saddened to say that tailing, losing a tail, or even noticing a tail are not skills in my repertoire, but after that night I would make them so.

22

We drove to the church first so that I would get familiar with the area and then we took routes completely around the park. We made all the necessary turns and moves and found the circus. It was pretty simple actually. They had placed the semis, painted wagons, and trailers, on the outer edge of the camp. It was easy to see their advertising just by passing on the road. We took off and circled back to find the church.

My estimate of a quarter mile of woods through which to traipse might have been a little light. It was looking like closer to a full mile and it would be through thick trees. Luckily, both of our phones had compass apps and if they failed, Bullfinch had an actual compass with him. We drove from the church back into York and stopped at a restaurant. I know what you're thinking. I'm always eating.

Hey, I just figure its best to go out on a full stomach. Besides that, we wanted to wait until it got closer to night fall. Sure the Koshii was a predator and thus more at home in the dark, but we weighed that against most of the camp being asleep. I wanted to avoid as many of the carnies as possible. The sun was a long way from setting and we'd need to kill some time. Besides that, we had never actually worked out how we were going to get the Koshii to come out to the woods. I didn't think I could put a baby on a string and pull it past his trailer.

Poor taste, I know, but hey, if I wasn't laughing I might be crying.

We ate our dinner and dragged out our coffee for as long as possible. Luckily, the place was pretty empty and the waitress didn't seem to be in a rush to get rid of us. We managed to kill a few hours.

"How the hell do we get him out of his trailer?" I asked as I sipped my coffee.

Bullfinch shook his head. "Perhaps a summoning of some sort?"

I sighed, I guess if I had to believe in monsters, I needed to believe in magic as well. "So now you're a professor and a wizard?"

He shook his head and smiled wryly, "No, I'm not a wizard and I probably couldn't do it. I do believe in the efficacy of certain charms and talismans however, and the strength of the written word. If the creature is sensitive, I might be able to draw a word of power that will call him forth." He sipped his tea.

"So our plan is, we get close, you draw a rune in the dirt and we hope that it makes him tingle and then… we have him?" I tried not to roll my eyes as I gulped down my coffee.

"Well, it's better than a putting a baby on a string," he said drily.

I choked and spit my coffee across half the table. He chuckled, I hadn't mentioned the baby on a string to him and I didn't expect his sense of humor to be similar to my own. I mopped the table clean and we shared a laugh.

"Maybe we could look up some words in Punjabi and literally call him out and to the woods?" I said.

Bullfinch gave me a slow shrug. I guess looking up curse words in a foreign language wasn't his idea of a good use of our time.

"Also, what if there are other… things… in the camp, what if something else feels your… charm?"

"I can't guarantee that others won't sense the charm. Hell, I can't even guarantee that the Koshii will. Sometimes you need faith. Do you know which of the wagons is his?"

"No, but I have it sort of narrowed down. There are several clearly marked… well, I hate to say this, but they are clown cars. So I know which ones are for the clowns. Also, I know one I'm certain is not his, because when I was there making a fuss last time, several clowns came out of it and he wasn't with them. He must have a small personal wagon. He never takes off his paint; I can't see him having a roommate."

"Well, it seems like it's the best we've got. We'll come in, we'll watch, and hopefully eliminate some of the others. At the least get it down to a handful and then we'll just have to go the Peeping Tom route. Perhaps we'll be able to simply knock on the door and invite him out for a rematch."

It was the best idea we had, so we lapsed into comfortable silence. We pushed the limit of the waitress's patience and when we left I made sure there was an ample tip left on the table.

We pulled into the church parking lot. I was pleased to see that there were no lights in the back half of the lot and what few cars had been there earlier had now left. The last minutes had been tense and quiet and I felt much better getting out of the car. I shook my legs, loosening the tension. My palms were damp with sweat. I think I'd been less nervous the first time I went inside. It was funny, as I was better prepared this time and had a partner, but I couldn't dismiss the churning in my guts.

I pulled the duffle out of the backseat and placed it on the hood. "Ready for the surprise?"

Bullfinch didn't say a word; he merely raised a single eyebrow and waited. I reached into the bag and pulled out the shotgun.

"Specially loaded shells with ash shaving and double ought buck. Probably only good at extremely close range, but should be a hell of an equalizer." I held it out for him. Before he could take it a voice cut through the moment.

"I knew that face was same and I knew you would return here when I saw you circle the lot. Perhaps you not get the message first time. You cause lots of trouble for us." The voice was a grumbling burr, mechanical and resonating, and I knew who it was instantly. Lazlo.

All three of us froze for a second. Calculating. I opened my mouth to speak, managed to say, "Wait…" before the giant was moving. I dropped the shotgun and grabbed the end of one of the bats; it was one of the studded ones. I charged into Lazlo, dropping beneath his huge swinging fist as I smashed the bat into his left knee.

He wobbled for a second and then slammed into the hood of my car. I winced as the grille cracked and the shotgun slid off the hood with a squeal like nails on a chalkboard. Note to self, *get a shitty car that I don't care about for future missions.*

Bullfinch stepped in and side-kicked the damaged knee. It was a neat and efficient strike that told me all my guesses had been correct. The professor knew how to handle himself. Lazlo should have been down; he should have been bawling that his ACL and MCL were destroyed. Instead, he was grumbling like a warthog. He grabbed the front of Bullfinch's jacket and pulled him close and then shoved him away with a shake of his head.

I didn't really want to have to do anything permanent to the guy. Sure, he was a thug, but he thought he was doing good and he was right that I had ruined their New York Shows. The knee should have had him down, but it didn't, so I had to step up my game.

"Look Lazlo, you really don't want to do this. I'm not here to make trouble."

The huge Gypsy looked at the shotgun on the ground and the bat in my hand and then charged me again. Big but not stupid. I grabbed the bat with both hands and gave it a full swing. I hit him so hard that I was afraid the bat would shatter on his face. Heat flashed across my own cheek and I stepped back from the weaving giant. It was like the itch, but the itch hadn't come back since Roland had touched me. The heat throbbed in my cheek and as I stepped further back, the throb diminished. At least it was less annoying than the itch.

"You gonna give…?" I meant to finish with "it up" but I was staggered by the sight before me. I had laid open Lazlo's cheek, the skin flapping down, and I could see the gleam of teeth and metal… but not a drop of blood. "Am I fighting the Terminator?"

There was a clicking noise and then a crackle and Lazlo straightened up, his tiny eyes opening wide. He swung around, revealing Bullfinch and the tiny stun gun he held, the clicking of the electricity arcing between the poles. Lazlo hammered a fist into Bullfinch's chest and the older man crumbled back and landed against my car. The blow should have broken ribs, but Bullfinch merely grunted and shook his head, slightly winded. Was the guy wearing body armor under his tweed jacket?

I winced. I needed to get the fighting away from my car. I dropped the bat and ran at Lazlo. He swung around and I grabbed his arm, dropping him to the ground. I pulled hard and no matter what he was, his joints worked the same as anyone else's, so his body followed the arm. He flipped over and landed on his back and I scrambled over him to put him into an arm bar. I pulled with all my strength and felt the arm loosen in the socket, then break across both the ulna and radius. Lazlo squealed. He could feel pain and now that my panic was lowering, I was wondering if perhaps the metal I had seen was merely some bridgework? Then again, he still wasn't bleeding. He was also trying to pull the arm out of my grasp; no normal person would do that. The arm should have been limp and useless and yet it was taking all I had to hold it in place.

Suddenly Bullfinch was there, grabbing a handful of Lazlo's hair and pulling it away from his face. He frowned, apparently not liking what he saw, or perhaps what he didn't see. I struggled to maintain my hold on the arm. It was disgusting as the forearm just wriggled and moved unnaturally in my sweaty grasp.

Bullfinch ripped Lazlo's shirt open and smiled. What the hell? He licked his palm and smeared the saliva on the man's chest. Lazlo shuddered. What the hell? Then he just went limp, the rumbling purr going out of his chest.

Bullfinch stood and wiped his palm on his pants, grimacing in clear disgust. I disengaged from the giant and stood, still clueless as to just what had happened.

"You are the most interesting person I have ever met, Mr. Shaw. You make friends with reincarnated heroes, hunt down immortal monsters from legend, and then have a golem attack you. Are you going to open a path to Faerie next?" I think that last was his idea of a joke. I don't know.

"You mean like the Jewish clay man thing, golem, that golem? Yeah, I'm just a barrel of laughs and good times. But what about you? Are you hiding body armor under there? How are those ribs?" He ignored my questions, scribbling notes into a notebook, so I crouched and looked over Lazlo. The beard was a fake, glued on to a face made out of cured leather and it was large and bushy enough to hide a speaker in the throat. The grumbling purr literally was from a mechanical device creating sounds within the chest. I didn't want to know how the rest worked.

"You know the myth; surprising." I tried not to be insulted. "Yes, *that* golem, though looking him over, he does not appear to be made of clay but rather of leather over perhaps a steel and wooden frame. It's truly fascinating."

"Understatement. Lazlo was a brute, but he had a personality and could think and reason. He was a person for all intents and purposes. I don't know if I want to know how it was done. Did you kill him?" I stepped away from the inert golem.

"Perhaps. I really don't know. The golem is activated by a single syllable *Aleph* drawn on it. In this case it was on his chest. Perhaps I merely need to return the word to him and he will rise again, or perhaps he will have to be recreated by the rabbi who made him. I don't really know and I'm not really concerned about it. We have a mission. As to my resilience, while you prepared weapons I readied my defenses." He picked up the shotgun and the baseball bats and returned them to the hood of the car. He didn't explain anything further.

"Well, help me drag him into the trees. We don't want him discovered while we're out in the field." I grabbed the arms and started to pull. Bullfinch joined and we managed to muscle the bulk into the trees.

I returned to the hood of car, looking over the scratched paint and the broken grille. I sighed. I pulled on my MMA gloves and then put my twin studded bats into a shotgun scabbard over my shoulder. I grabbed the bag with the extra ammo and Bullfinch took his bat, the shotgun, and the spear-point bat.

We entered the woods without further comment and checked our phones to get our bearings. West and slightly south and we'd arrive at the campground. As we got closer I thought about the itch, now a hot throbbing, in my cheek. I was marked by the Koshii and that mark was apparently reacting to the presence of supernatural threats. The closer Lazlo came to me the more my cheek had throbbed. The itch changed to a throb after the touch of Roland, who admitted he could relive the moment of my scarring and who I firmly believed was the reincarnation of a mythical hero.

I mulled it over for a while and then finally decided to break our silence.

"I think Roland did something to me. The scar—it reacts when we're near anything unnatural. We might be able to find the Koshii merely by getting close to it." We pushed on and before long we could make out the lights of the campground. We had strayed slightly further than we intended and it was only a matter of moments before we were sitting at the edge of the trees and spying down on a mass of campers and trucks. I could see the pickup from earlier, which meant that after leaving Lazlo to wait for me, the driver had rushed back to the camp. I wondered if Ben and bunch of Gypsies were headed to the church, or worse, combing through the woods.

There was a lot of activity in the camp, several large fires and apparently some of the acts were practicing. I could see tumblers and acrobats working out in the grass, people singing and playing instruments, food and drink being passed around. It was a full-blown party and my heart sank. I had little hope that everyone would decide that it was time for bed, all of them at exactly 10 PM. I settled back and tried to think this through. It was confusing, why was everyone partying when the truck driver had to have alerted the camp?

I voiced my doubts to Bullfinch.

"Perhaps it's merely a method of control. Ben and his men are looking for you, but they don't want the rest of the camp up in arms or worried. Especially as they have no proof you're really here. So the rest of the camp parties on and only a select few are alert. Either way, we need to keep our eyes open and proceed with care."

"Do you think we should just come back closer to morning? I think they'll be going long into the night."

Bullfinch crouched beside me but didn't answer. He was looking through the crowds. Finally he gestured toward one knot of people. "There, the clowns are practicing as well. Perhaps if we circle around slightly, we'll get close enough and I can try to pull him." He finally answered my question, talking over his shoulder as we edged through the brush to get a better view. "In the time I've spent with you I've determined you are a fairly headstrong individual. To be honest, I think you act far too hastily, and while I find it a good sign that you're starting to think it through now, I think it best to act. They might be pulling up camp come morning."

I nodded as I took in his words. He was right, we were here and we were ready. I looked where he was pointing and sure enough, I saw some men, most of them out of makeup but a few still in their full get-up. They were practicing their pratfalls and other foolery. We edged around and I got a little closer. Then I froze, grabbing Bullfinch's sleeve. He looked at me and then followed my gaze.

"He's right there," I whispered, despite the fact that we were several hundred feet away and the music and yelling easily covered any sound I could have made.

"How can you be sure? There are many who are still wearing their makeup."

My cheek throbbed slightly, a whisper of a touch of heat, "I know, and besides I'd never forget that face. Clowns register their faces you know, they're trademarked." I glared at the clown. I wanted him to sense my hate. I wanted to will him to come over.

Bullfinch grunted and then began to clear a patch of earth. He drew a circle in the ground with his finger tip and muttered some words under his breath. I was about to make a comment about the absurdity of his idea when I felt a flash of heat across my face. I looked to the Koshii but he still stood on the edge of the group of clowns. Bullfinch slashed another figure into the circle and I felt another flash of heat up my cheek. I had no answer for that, but was glad I hadn't voiced my disdain again.

He finished his figures and then he placed his palm on the circle and spoke a single word. I still have no clue what it was and I haven't wanted to ask since then. The energy that came from that small circle was real, and it rolled over me and down across the field. I held my breath and wondered if he could see or sense us. I felt the burn across my cheek and my fear that others would feel it returned. I was certain that we had just launched the magical equivalent of a flare. However, nothing changed below. The music and dancing didn't stop, but then the Koshii stumbled and turned his gaze directly on us.

The Koshii turned to some of the other clowns. He shook his head, gestured with his hands, and then walked away from the mass. He stumbled again as he walked deeper into the camp, then I lost sight of him. I cursed softly as he got further away from us. He disappeared back toward his wagon, or so I assumed.

"Great, it drove him away. What the heck do we do now?"

"Circle and follow, or perhaps I can do it again. It is rather crude, saying he even felt it." Bullfinch erased his markings.

"I'm sure he felt it. *I* felt it." I moved into an easy jog as I tried to keep the disappearing Koshii in sight. Our best bet was to follow him toward his home and then get him out of there.

I was moving faster than a jog when I felt a flash of heat. I dropped to the ground. It probably saved my life, as a long, wavy blade hissed through the air and took a chunk of bark out of a tree. I felt another flush of heat and scrambled to my feet. The Koshii was coming right at me, a nearly two-foot-long kris blade in his hand as he thrust for my heart.

I stepped forward, turned my body, and sent my left arm to deflect the blade and my right fist toward the demon's face. Several ounces of lead should stagger it back even if it wouldn't harm its skin.

My hands encountered nothing and I staggered. What? Then I remembered that Koshii liked illusions. The last time I fought him everything had seemed distorted, he'd been hitting me with the minor mojo, but now he was coming on full force. A length of silk slithered across my throat and suddenly I was no longer thinking about illusions or how much the monster might fear me. I was more worried about breathing.

The silk scarf tightened fast and I was already losing my vision. I threw elbows back into the monster and dropped down, trying to throw it over my shoulder. It was a no go, the Koshii was far stronger than me and he merely jerked me back, my feet leaving the ground and things cracking in my neck. I was terrified and tried very hard not to piss my pants.

Bullfinch erupted from the cover of a bush, both hands loaded with supplies because I hadn't been smart enough to grab an extra shotgun scabbard for my partner. Thankfully, he seemed possessed of preternatural calm. He dropped the shotgun—which would have done more harm to me than our foe—and the spear, coming at the Koshii with his scuffed bat.

The Koshii turned into the blow, trying to use me as a shield. I had time to bite back the scream as the bat slammed into my shoulder. Luckily, the trick joint didn't slip and better yet, the bat still managed to strike the Koshii as well.

It grunted and the silk loosened around my neck. Blessed air filled my lungs and I stomped on the oversize clown shoe, hoping to find flesh and bone in the padding. The Koshii pulled its foot back, its balance shifting and I dropped to the ground, throwing it over my shoulder. I was free.

Bullfinch smacked it twice with his bat and the Koshii scrambled away, cursing in a language I didn't recognize. Then again, I was not really concerned with what he was saying. I merely translated it into a series of curse words. The thing kicked Bullfinch in the knee and then scrambled to its feet and took off. As it ran, it divided into three images and I shook my head. Heat flared across my cheek again and I clamped my right eye shut and looked through the left. Two of the images wavered but one remained solid.

I took off after the real Koshii and was pleased to see Bullfinch hobbling after. We wove through the trees, further and further away from the camp. The Koshii glanced back and tried his trick two more times, but as long as I squinted my left eye, I could see through the illusions.

I grunted, as a tree branch slapped me in the face. It was a good thing I ran a lot or else he would have gotten away easily. As it was, the Koshii was gaining ground. I couldn't think of what to do and with nothing else making sense I drew one of the bats off my back and hurled it toward the Koshii's knees.

Luck or divine favor, the clown dropped and rolled and I put on a new burst of speed. I leapt forward and went into a roll, picking up my dropped bat and then I closed on the creature as it stood.

Both bats whipping through the air, I struck it in the jaw and throat and the Koshii dropped back, spitting blood and choking.

I felt a surge of pure primal savagery tear through me. All the anger and pain roared out of me in a rush. I struck again and again, the Koshii cursing me in that ancient language, as I wove through its counterattacks and delivered rapid strikes all over its body.

I wondered where the hell Bullfinch was and it was the only mistake I made. I let my concentration break for just a moment. The Koshii got its hands on me. The bat in my left hand was wrenched away and a stiff arm smashed into my chest. I flew back and struck a tree, pain flashing across my back, sharp and intense in my lower left side as I pushed off the tree. Something snagged my clothes and I faltered as I tried to pull free.

Cloth tore and I staggered forward, directly into my own studded bat, which was swinging directly into my face. I dropped and rolled across the clearing, spots dancing before my eyes and the pain in my back trebled. I felt wet warmth and wondered just what had snagged me.

I was glad to see that the Koshii was breathing hard. I got back to my feet, using the bat as a crutch until I could stand again. I held the bat up in one hand and pointed it toward my foe. He sneered at me and drew the kris knife from his belt into one hand. He held the bat in the other. The bastard was going to use my own style against me.

I feinted with the bat and when he raised his weapons to block, I twirled my wrist and struck him in the chest. He snarled and lunged forward, his bat swinging to take my head off and I leaned away. The knife went for my gut and I spun away from that as well, hammering the bottom of my bat against the Koshii's wrist. His hand sprang open and the knife tumbled through the air.

I turned to follow its path and the Koshii body checked me. I hit the ground and rolled, my back tearing more and more blood flowing free. I was seriously screwed and didn't know how I was going to pull out of this one. Where the hell was Bullfinch?

My thoughts were answered. He stumbled into the clearing and leveled the shotgun. The Koshii looked up with a sneer and

Bullfinch pulled the trigger. I don't know who was more surprised, me or the clown. He hit the ground with a scream, blood pouring out of his stomach and over his silk clothes. It started to rise and Bullfinch chambered another round and calmly stepped closer. He blasted out the right kneecap. Slide and chamber. Blasted out the left knee.

Very calmly he rolled the gun over and began to reload, pulling shells off a sling on the stock that held nine rounds. He finished the load and chambered a round and brought the gun to his cheek, he waited.

The Koshii mewed, it was a pathetic sound and I didn't feel an ounce of sympathy. The creature had existed for millennia eating people, cheating the years to stay young. He had eaten a small boy, missing his front teeth, who only wanted to make his mom happy and maybe get a trip to the circus.

I limped over to Bullfinch and pulled the sharpened bat out of his belt. I staggered over to the Koshii.

"You were right before. I didn't know what I was messing with, but then, neither did you. I only know about two of your victims and that was two too many. You're a tough bastard, Mr. Koshii," the creature's eyes widened and he bared his teeth at me. "You see, now I know what you are and now I know that Ash can hurt you. I hope that Ravanna is waiting for you in hell."

I more fell than thrust, but either way the bat slid through his guts and into the ground beneath him. My two hundred plus pounds of muscle were more than enough to get the job done. As the bat slid through him the Koshii growled, "Screw you…."

Then he thrashed and froze, muscles cramped tight into a rigid knot. I gasped and fell over beside him and woke a second later as Bullfinch tore my shirt off and started doing something to my back.

Whatever it was, it hurt like hell and the next thing I knew, he was applying pressure and rolling me over to sit up. I grunted and protested, trying to push him off.

"Koshii, we gotta finish it," I managed to say while gasping at the pain.

"It's not going anywhere. It's paralyzed but you might bleed to death." He wrapped the long silk scarf around my waist and pulled it tight, maintaining the pressure on my back.

"Did you just use my shirt as a bandage and then tie it off with the strangle scarf?"

"It's called a Rumel and was the preferred method of assassination among the Thuggee Cult." He began to scrape a clear area, tossing aside branches and dry leaves.

"Thanks for the lesson, Prof." I tried to help as best I could, but I could barely get up under my own power. I just pushed dirt around with my feet and then finally crawled out of the area as Bullfinch pulled the body into the freshly cleared earth. He stood back and eyed his work.

"What took you so long?" I asked.

"I had to go back for the shotgun and spear. You took off so fast and I went right after you, leaving everything behind." He reached into a breast pocket of his coat and pulled out his pipe. I laughed and he shook his head as he pulled out a pouch with tobacco and a small bottle with a flip top. He put all but the small bottle back into his pocket and then he popped the top and flicked out a single, strike-anywhere match. With a practiced flick he lit the match with his thumbnail and dropped it onto the Koshii.

True to the book, the creature instantly ignited into flames without any accelerant.

The heat washed over me and I smiled. Bullfinch helped me to my feet and we watched the corpse burn. It went more quickly than I would have thought. Burning super hot. We had to shy away from the flames.

Nothing but a deformed skeleton remained an hour later and we went and shattered the bones with our bats and spread the dust. I had no energy left. I was spent. I left the bats behind in the woods and slipped the shotgun into the now empty scabbard.

We found our bearings and, without a backward glance, hobbled back to the car.

23

I was glad it was over; at least, I hoped it was over. We limped out of the woods to find Lazlo laid out in front of the car. I remembered dragging him back into the trees, and I stopped cold. I started to swear and I stepped away from Bullfinch. I reached for the shotgun over my shoulder and heard the very loud click of a hammer being drawn back.

"Keep the hand well away from there." I put my hands up and out and felt someone yanking the shotgun off my back.

HH appeared at the hood of my car. I had the feeling that he might have been standing there the whole time but I just hadn't noticed him. He stepped closer to me, enough that I could make him out in the moonlight. He looked very upset.

Ben came out from behind me, a coach gun in one hand and my shotgun in the other. He handed my gun over to HH and kept the coach gun trained on me. I couldn't help but stare at the two huge barrels.

"So, you have returned to visit more misfortune upon me, Mitch?" I blinked, who the hell was Mitch? Then I remembered that was the name I told HH when I first found the circus. He had a good memory. "You have cost me much monies, much prestige. I have had to lie to some of my peoples; is very disconcerting to me. I abhor lies and even though I know you name not Mitch, is lie. I accept that you not want to give me real one. I understand the power of names. But now you cost me Lazlo, he been with circus for many decades and I know he hurt you, but still…" he shook his head and then looked closer at my face.

"Benji! What is this!?" he gestured to my cheek and I felt a slight flush of warmth. Interesting.

"I know not sir. I told the men just a slight beating, to scare him off."

I put my hands down. I was lightheaded and chilly without a shirt on, and I needed to see a doctor. "You had another werewolf of Hamburg."

That startled both of them. I staggered past them and sat on the hood of my car. I started to talk about a clown who hunted and ate children. I described his face and told them to check out his caravan. I was sure they would find something.

Bullfinch went to the car as soon as the guns were lowered and pulled out another bag. It contained medical supplies. I dry swallowed four Ibuprofen and then rolled over onto my stomach as I saw him pulling out needle and thread.

"How do you know of the werewolf?" was their first question, despite that I'd just told them that a clown was killing children.

"We ran into the Paladins. They said you sometimes mistakenly trust the worst people." I grunted as I felt the needle punching into my back.

"The good news is it looks like the cut is only muscle, a flesh wound. It doesn't look like anything vital has been pierced." Bullfinch was trying to be reassuring, but it wasn't helping.

HH and Ben talked quietly with each other in what I assumed was Hungarian and I faded out of the conversation for a few minutes as Bullfinch finished stitching my back.

"So this Koshii is now gone?" HH asked me finally.

"Dead and gone, never to trouble another child again." I rolled back over and felt a tremble turn my limbs to jelly. My body had reached its limit; I was done.

HH reached into his vest and pulled out a flask. He took a small sip and then held the bottle to me. It was full of schnapps and I took a huge slug out of the bottle, hoping that some numbing heat would get into my body and dull the various pains.

HH took the flask back and then gestured to Lazlo. "Payment enough for the beating and the other such, our debts are clear, peace between us." He held out his hand and I took it. I didn't have the energy to have another fight, especially when they had two shotguns and I was too slow to pull my pistol out of the shoulder rig. HH handed me the shotgun and then stepped back away from the car.

"You need to drive," I told Bullfinch and I limped around the car and fell into the passenger seat. He shrugged and took the driver seat. That was the last thing I was aware of until we arrived at my office.

24

That was the end of my first case and should have been the sec- ond time at the hospital. But Bullfinch had done a good job on my back and I was so beat up that once I got us past security and into the house, I just went back to sleep.

I woke hours later and Bullfinch was sitting at my desk.

"Well Jon, I'm glad you're finally awake. I thought it would be rude to just let myself out and I don't know how to arm your security systems. I've left some numbers here in case you have anything you aren't comfortable facing alone thrust upon you again. Maybe next time I'll merely help in a research capacity." He smiled and chuckled at his own joke and I grinned as well. My body felt like beaten leather. I staggered to my feet and limped my way into the bathroom, where I pulled an old bottle of Percocet off the shelf and swallowed one of the pills. I hated taking them and they were left over because I had only taken half as many as the doctor wanted me to.

I returned to the room. Bullfinch had literally packed and cleaned my desk. I can only imagine his level of boredom as I slept. I pulled open the top drawers. He had put my gun and holster back in the top right drawer and hadn't messed with the other weapons inside. I nodded.

"You're really itching to leave so fast? I was thinking we could have some more Indian food, maybe celebrate with a few beers." I headed into the kitchen and stopped dead. He had cleaned my kitchen as well. He really was bored.

"My ride is already on the way. It was a hell of a time, Jon. Hopefully it won't happen again, at least not too soon." I came back into the room and shook his hand.

"Yeah, thanks. I have to say it's pretty amazing what you and your people do. I mean, that guy on the computer is scary. You ever need anything, and I mean *anything*, I owe you. You need guns or explosives or another soldier, you give me a call and I'll be there."

"Thank you Jon, we will be in touch if the need should arise. I think you're going to have your hands full, though, if the Paladins are moving through here and into Mass. We'll be keeping an eye on HH and his circus." He shook my hand again and then reached for his bags.

"Hey, you gotta tell me about that defense thing you did, the body armor? How come Lazlo didn't shatter your ribs and the Koshii only bruised your knee?"

He shook his head and gave a slight smile. It was rather boyish on his face. "Trade secrets, Jon, and I don't have much time. I might be able to send you a book, though."

Then he turned, and was gone. Just like that, it was over. I stood on my porch drinking a Guinness and wondering just what I had gotten myself involved with. As I walked back into the house I stopped to look at the movie poster I'd had made. It had been such a joke when I first thought it up. But now it had become the truth.

I had to make a phone call. Erin needed to know that it was over.

I was Jon Shaw, Monster Hunter.

About the Author

Kurt M. Criscione **is a New England native;** his mother was born on Friday the 13th and his father was born on Halloween, while he was born on Thursday the 12th. He was raised by his mother on a steady diet of horror and big monster movies. A child of the 80s, he is a massive fan of Gaming and Ancient Myths/literature and an amateur Historian. He currently lives in Connecticut with his cat and is pursing his MFA in English/ Creative Writing.

CROSSROAD
PRESS

www.ingramcontent.com/pod-product-compliance
Lightning Source LLC
Chambersburg PA
CBHW072238190626
46809CB00018B/2844

* 9 7 8 1 9 4 8 9 2 9 3 4 9 *